THE AGE OF INFIDELITY

THE AGE
of
INFIDELITY

— *and other stories* —

Valerie Sayers

THE AGE OF INFIDELITY AND OTHER STORIES

Slant Books
P.O. Box 60295
Seattle, WA 98160

www.slantbooks.com

HARDCOVER ISBN: 978-1-63982-049-8
PAPERBACK ISBN: 978-1-63982-048-1
EBOOK ISBN: 978-1-63982-050-4

Cataloguing-in-Publication data:

Names: Sayers, Valerie.
Title: The ageof infidelity and other stories / Valerie Sayers.
Description: Seattle, WA: Slant Books, 2020 | Includes bibliographical references and index.
Identifiers: ISBN 978-1-63982-049-8 (hardcover) | ISBN 978-1-63982-048-1 (paperback) | ISBN 978-1-63982-050-4 (ebook)
Subjects: LCSH: Short stories, American | English -- fiction -- Short -- stories | United States -- Social life and customs -- 20th century -- Fiction.
Classification: PS3569.A94 A7 2020 (print) | PS3569.A94 (ebook)

Manufactured in the U.S.A.   OCTOBER 12, 2021

For Lillian Bayer and Jill Godmilow

CONTENTS

SUICIDE DOGS

ONCE UPON A TIME we haven't yet lived through—but I know we will, and you know it too—I moved to the outskirts of Greenglass with my young son and daughter. Their father had left us and I decided, under the circumstances, that we'd be better off a little distance from neighbors who were trying to scope out anything they could report to the Constitutional Guards. Besides, I thought we could plant a little garden to supplement the scant supplies I was allowed.

As you can guess, the garden didn't work out. That first summer I had only a handful of baby lettuces to gather before the rains streamed down and the river rose up: the landscape is flat and I was flooded sure as everybody else. The world was so wet that July I thought I was seeping out of my own body, my eyes and ears leaking day and night. I couldn't help but wonder if it was some new punishment they'd dreamed up.

One day when the rain and the hail pelted down together, the children and I heard a peculiar rustling outside. I cracked the front door open and watched a scruffy creature shake herself under what was left of our awning: she was a midsize mutt, her hair neither short nor long but thick and yellow, red-tinged, matted with rain. When I opened the door a little wider, against my better judgment, the dog made a dignified promenade into our little front room and proceeded to lay herself down on the straw mat as if she'd lived with us forever. She cocked her head to one side, awaiting further instructions.

Well, you know about children and yellow dogs. Pete and Annie gazed on her with reverence. I made the usual objections—that her people must be looking, that we barely had enough food for ourselves—but I knew from the first that she had joined our exile. You have to respect a dame who just strolls in and makes herself at home. We called her Ruby.

* * *

That same summer Pete witnessed his first dog suicide. One afternoon when the rain let up, he went on a ramble through the remaining woods and on his way home saw another yellow dog biding his time by the side of the road. Rabies was rampant again, so he hung back.

"He was waiting for a truck to come fast."

"Pete, sweetie, we can't know that."

"I know. I watched him. He was looking up and down the road."

"I bet lots of trucks passed."

"They were too slow. You know, you know what I mean."

Pete was only seven that year, still young enough to let me touch him, still beautiful. He was the opposite of me: serious, responsible. His dark hair climbed up his forehead before it fell back down, and the freckles on his cheeks matched the walnut shade of his curls. He said this dog stood patient as a guard on duty while the slow convoys ambled through, but soon as he heard the rumble of the solo truck racing to catch up, he crouched and sprang. The driver didn't stop, so it was up to my little boy to drag the mangled oozing body from the asphalt to the ditch. The buzzards were circling by the time he headed home.

I scrubbed him up, down, and sidewise, but he said he'd watched the dog long enough to be sure: no foaming, nothing strange.

"Nothing strange but throwing himself in front of a truck."

So I suppose I was beginning to believe it even then. Ruby sat quiet, listening to his story while I cleaned the blood and the goo at the kitchen sink.

* * *

You know exactly what happened next: years of drought followed the rains, and after three of those years I saw what foolishness it was to think I'd ever have a garden of greens again, much less a blooming fruit tree. I taught the children how to juice the cacti they planted by the side of the road: Guard Juice, we called it, and gurgled to signify our contempt. Pete and Annie roamed while they still could, in the early morning and the late afternoon, their sun gear weighing them down. The guards didn't bother children, only to ask whether they'd seen anyone hiding, and my children knew to shake their heads no without a single word. No wiseguy business—thank God, they weren't born with my wise-guy gene.

One suppertime they brought a friend they found in their roaming into the shade of our little house. The three of them had seen another dog lunge into a fast convoy and language streamed out of them: not appalled exactly, just excited, the way we all get when we watch disaster happen. Pete had seen plenty more dogs fling themselves at trucks in those three years, but he was getting old enough to doubt his own eyes. This time he had witnesses.

Their new friend Jude said: "Your dog saw too." I calculated Jude to be between Pete and Annie's ages, maybe eight or nine, with the look of a cartoon bird: he worried his lower lip in and out as if he were about to open his beak for food. "She was talking, it was like talking, and then she growled. When that other dog got hit." Ruby sat tall and held herself perfectly still, listening.

Nothing to do, I thought, but offer this birdchild supper while they all calmed down. We still had some of the plantains and yucca the children were allotted. We'd make it a little party, and Ruby could lick our plates. We messaged Jude's mother on his wristie and she beamed back: "MAY I TALK TO YOU PRIVATELY."

So I asked Jude if I could borrow his wristie. He unstrapped it right away but as I went off to the kitchen, flinging a scarf around my neck, I heard him whisper: "Where's your wristies, guys? Where's hers?"

And even before I saw his mother's small face, birdlike too, pinched on the little childsize screen, I knew it was dangerous to talk to her in my condition, crazy lonely, disguising myself with scarves. Be good, I told myself, which was how I always knew I was about to be bad. I craved the company of women enough to do something foolish, whereas I avoided men and stayed out of trouble. Who wouldn't, after the children's father who couldn't contain his jealousy, after the guards who stripped me naked, after the judge who took my device away and said I was unfit for the company of decent citizens. His kind of decency I could do without—but I did long for another woman, one who would chatter, tell me a new joke, repeat Guard-gossip. We could dance! I was getting carried away.

"You're kind to have Jude over." She stared at me so intently I began to blink. "We can't afford, he's not in school."

I let myself hope, just a little. Most folks couldn't afford to send their children to school anymore, but that phrase—we can't afford, the *it* lopped off—was the code schoolies used. I said: "Me too. I can't afford."

[3]

She tapped the air where she saw Jude's ID code in the corner. "You can't afford a device, either."

She was either rude as she could be or she'd guessed the truth. I felt myself throwing off all good sense, the way you do when you fall in love. I didn't even know her name. "It was taken."

Only those three words: it sounded like I was talking about my virginity. The notion scared a laugh out of me, after what I'd been through, but when I heard the sound of my own giggle, creaky and out of practice, I knew what level of mistake I'd made. She was still staring.

"You're on home exile."

I didn't say a word. I stared back, into the little wristie I held at arm's length, but I couldn't help feeling to see if my scarf was still in place. Maybe I could make home exile look fashionable?

"I'll come right away. If I'm stopped, I'll say you're my sister."

I tried to sound breezy: "The court says I'm allowed visitors." I didn't let on how few visitors I'd had, how long ago.

"They changed the rules. Only family allowed now."

Without a wristie I had no way to receive the message about my new punishment. Boy, the Constitutional Authority really didn't know how to take a joke. I pictured the long list of things I didn't know, cut off like this. What if the bond I'd posted to pay for my supplies wasn't enough anymore? What if they tried to take my children? Those words, *my children*, must have escaped.

She was as no-nonsense as a third-grade teacher. "They're OK. Now stop, please, and delete all that."

Both wristie screens went blank as I followed her command. I knew a lot of women like her, Midwestern women who specialized in nice but knew the way the world worked, who told you that dress made you look fat, that if you could just pick up the dustballs the clutter wouldn't matter so much, that you shouldn't stick your neck out.

Ruby wandered in and stood next to me, ears pricked, listening to the erasure of my conversation. She was a strange mix of breeds, the long collie snout rounding out over fierce jaws, her ribs showing but her muscles rippling. Since the day she arrived, she'd taken in every word, every pitch of our voices. My head swam off into some dead gray horizon. They couldn't listen to every conversation, God knows, but what if they'd caught ours? They might take Jude's mother away too, and I didn't even know yet if she'd tell me my man-size shirt from the charity pile at Supply Distribution didn't flatter me.

Ruby nudged the back of my knee, as if to say: *Buck up.*

* * *

I waited for Jude's mother by the window, where I hadn't let myself stand for the longest time—the landscape had been erased so systematically I preferred to imagine the old one. Even before it declined into a sad rustbelt city, nobody would have called this city beautiful, but here and there, especially on the outskirts, a simple green charm as unsophisticated as the rest of the Midwest once defined us. Now those trees had all withered or died: sycamores and pin oaks, black walnuts and mulberries, even the spindly honeysuckle that used to drape itself so carelessly over the roadway from here to town, turning a springtime walk dappled and dreamy. Now animals choked on the gristle of poisonous plants they couldn't smell anymore. The children said Ruby chewed off dangling saplings and used them for bones. Her jaws are pit bull, I told them: those dogs chew through metal.

It was cheaper for the Authority if I raised my children myself, so the first ten years of my sentence was home exile, mother's exemption. After that, when Annie turned twelve, I was supposed to report for hard labor—but I would never leave my children alone in this cottage to fend for themselves. It would be safest to escape in year seven or eight: I concocted plans on a daily basis. We would make our way to the riverbed by night—the children told me it was dried to a trickle—and follow it north until the trickle gurgled into a stream.

The plans fell apart as the landscape disappeared, as remains of trees and bushes blew or rolled or burned away, as the hiding places thinned and evaporated. We had no vehicle, no scrip card, no communications device. Sometimes my scheme involved a birchbark canoe, but that would require a birch tree, and finding one was as unlikely as dancing with a stranger. Anyway, the biggest obstacle was my tracking collar.

Ruby stretched out on her own belly, her long face focused on me as I gazed in turn at the exposed road twenty yards from my front window. Finally Jude's mother came into view, a slight figure holding up a sun hat with a twelve-inch brim. Witches' hats, the children called them. At least no Guards showed themselves. When I held the door open she flew inside, as bossypants as she'd been on the phone.

"How do you do. I must collect my son."

I heard my voice come out as high-pitched as the children's, telling her how Jude had come to be in an exile's house. Fool that I am, I still held out hope: I told Jude's mother how the children tried to stop the dog from flinging itself under the truck. She nodded as if she'd heard it a thousand times.

"An epidemic. Our neighbor's Pekinese leapt from their roof."

"My God!"

"God had nothing to do with it." She shook her head without a hint of humor. "She had to climb out a little dormer window. Must have slid it open with her nose."

"I never heard of such a thing."

"Then you haven't heard about that mother and son—Dobermans, of all the breeds—that had to pry the Oxycodone out of the tin where they were hidden."

"The CG still allows Oxy?"

"Are you kidding? Basic necessity. Especially for a dog who wants to kill herself."

The sound of her voice! She chattered on about dog suicides, gazing all round the cottage, looking for her son. She'd pushed her sunguards up atop her hat and I saw why her stare had appeared so intense: her eyes were bright and dark, a little too small even for so small a face. She held them open extra-wide to compensate. I held out a hand to take her sunrobe, hoping against hope that she would linger, but she shook her head and pulled the robe tighter over her blaster. It shouldn't have shocked me. Everybody has to carry one.

"I really must go."

Why had I deluded myself? Even the distributors at the supply center knew better than to speak to a woman with the collar. If this were a happier story I'd say that one or two of them tried to smile at me surreptitiously, but they most certainly did not, they clicked their tongues and made hissing noises even when they saw the children blushing. And now this skinny small-eyed woman who'd been decent to me for ten seconds stretched her neck out, scanning, terrified to stay one minute longer in my fairytale cottage. I touched her forearm and watched her jump:

"What's happening to the dogs?"

"The heat's so hard on them. We're all so thirsty." She couldn't stop herself even as she pulled her arm back. "Nobody tells jokes anymore. Nobody sings." Nobody dances! She'd read my mind. Her voice raised ever so slightly, enough for her little boy to come running.

Before I even had time to ask whether the children could meet Jude outside the house again sometime, to promise that I wouldn't go near them, they were vaporizing, vanishing from our lives as quickly as they'd come. I stood by the window and watched them fade down that desolate road, stripped even of the mourning doves that used to wake us.

And felt, yes, desolate myself: yes, broken. I felt defiant too. The Stricters think home exile is the most effective way to break your spirit, but they forgot to calculate how a woman with children and a dog could hang on to something like cussedness even after the charges piled up. I admit forthrightly that spray-painting on the old railroad trestles was juvenile—worse than juvenile, since Pete would never do such a thing. I guess it wasn't polite, either, to tell that guard his weaponry was compensatory, but who knew we weren't allowed to psychoanalyze anymore? I knew myself how stupid it was to start that "Low T Is What We Need" campaign when the CGs were distributing testosterone door to door. Only I didn't intend to go to prison. I intended to escape with my children and build a birchbark canoe.

I sang the children to sleep every night. We told jokes all the time, how can you not, how can you be alive and not tell a joke. I see now that I have told this story to this point without a single joke, so here. Here is my children's favorite joke: *What will the space creatures say when they come to rescue us and see our sorry state?*

Give up?

We won't know what they're saying. They don't speak English.

Pete and Annie could laugh themselves silly, laugh through their noses and bark, roll on the floor with tears and snot streaming, Ruby romping between them, licking them clean. They'd spend the afternoon inventing space languages—*greenlich grinderhardling gro*—languages that sounded Germanic and philosophical, existentially inclined.

* * *

Another year passed the same: the heat seemed to stabilize, though that could have been my body adapting. The children did not see Jude again.

Annie was so lonely that she cuddled Ruby tight, till even Ruby squirmed free. Our dog seemed sadder, too, her tail pumping less. I didn't think she'd dart into traffic, but just the same we began to leash her with a rope. Sometimes she shuddered, as if in fear or disgust, and sometimes she rubbed herself desperately against the straw mat, working the rope we'd forgotten. Untying it, I told her: "I know all about that," and it seemed to me she regarded my tracking collar. Sisters under the skin.

Pete was quieter, too: I won't go so far as to say he was turning sullen, but he wanted to know why he couldn't petition to have a device. He hadn't done anything wrong. I hoped he hadn't heard, in his roaming, about the Low T campaign.

The day he asked me about a device was the day I decided: we had to leave soon, sooner than I'd planned. I didn't know how we could get more than a quarter-mile down the road and if we did, we'd only be looking for shelter, for one good soul to hide us until we could set out again and look for the next good soul, the soul who knew whether we should head north or east, whether the C.A. had taken Canada, whether Vermont was still resisting. We'd have to forage among new plants we didn't recognize and God only knew where we would find water. The guards would hear Ruby bark and shoot us on sight, or we would shrivel up like the scrub on some lonesome path. And anyway there was the collar. "Ruby," I said, "if you're chewing saplings in the woods . . ."

I suppose you think it's madness to talk that way to an animal. Riddle me this, then: the next morning I found her in my bed, cuddled close, gnawing at the thing. The timing wasn't quite right—she might have disrupted the transmission before we were ready—so I rose and said: "Soon, Ruby. Soon."

If we were going to escape, I had to speak more precisely.

* * *

One evening soon after, the children came running. Pete shushed Annie till the door was properly closed and led us away from the windows to the center hallway, a little old man in his cumbersome sun gear protecting us. From his pocket he withdrew a tiny strip of paper. When he thrust it out, Annie chirped that it came from Jude, that their friend wouldn't even talk to them. In tiny bird scratchings Jude's mother had written: *July 4 reverse day and night. Mandatory.*

Reverse day and night. That explained the signs in the Supply Center: DON'T FORGET the FOURTH. I'd taken them as the usual reminder to be our patriotic selves, to parade our weapons.

I led the children to the kitchen and gave them used cactus leaves to suck. I fetched Ruby a thimbleful of water. I sat myself at the table and pondered. Reverse day and night: meaning, I supposed, that here on in, everyone would work in the cooler nighttime, sleep in the day. It would be June in a matter of days, the last days we would have the cover of night. I heard myself say: "We have to leave tonight."

My children looked at me with their eyes half-closed, as if they were drifting off to sleep already at the enormity of it. I could barely open my own eyes, but I gathered up what we needed: a knife, our water bottles, three pieces of cloth for washing our bodies and our teeth if we were lucky enough to find water, Ruby's rope. I didn't even trouble with a scarf. "What about your necklace?" Annie said.

I found the last of the palm oil, and my children rubbed it into the back of my collar, and then Ruby got to work. I fretted that it would take all night, and we would have to leave by day, but she found the spot in the space of an hour. When the red light went out, we took her rope and ran. Let me hasten to add: we were not the Israelites fleeing by night, we were a mother too stupid to keep her mouth shut and her two children who hadn't done anything wrong.

* * *

She led us through the nights, Ruby who knew where the old paths were, Ruby whose barking came only by day now, as if she knew the cost. She caught us squirrels no bigger than mice and ate them so lustily that even Annie overcame her squeamishness. She stayed close enough to make us forget about the rope: we lost it somewhere past the Indiana border.

I counted the days as best I could, tearing the frayed hem of my sunrobe once for every blistering sunrise. We were already covered in grime from sleeping on what was left of field and woods. I calculated it was mid-June, and though it was slow going, we all grew stronger in the dark, moving faster as the land rolled and climbed. We reached the riverbanks, steep all around and stubbled with tree trunks, the riverbed itself caked mud sucking us down. The bats had gone the way of the bees, and so we were blistered with bug bites by the end of the first night.

What used to be the river headed north and so did we. When we began to see more glimpses of green, and the water flowed into a steady stream, it was hard to sleep by day. I stored up songs: "Which Side Are You On?" and "Stardust" and "Oh Mary, Don't You Weep," crazy hopeful mismatched songs from the long-ago past that I sang sotto voce by night, hoping my children could follow the beat. Soon we'd lose the cover of darkness. Soon we'd have to ask for help.

We were deep into Michigan by then. I was tempted to run, to reach water we could scoop up—the Great Lakes couldn't have dried up entirely, could they?—but we had to stay close and quiet. At points the river widened and then we had to scramble up those steep banks, more likely to spy critters than people moving about.

But I knew we were close, too, to where the militias had congregated in vast numbers. My children stopped whispering questions about where we were headed. I told them I didn't know if there'd be lakefront to walk: those rebels had brought the dunes down with their explosions. I didn't dare dream that we would cross all the way to Canada by foot, but I didn't dare not dream, either.

One night when we sensed we were coming very close to the lake, Ruby began to limp. I thought maybe she'd got a thorn in her paw. I'd brought only one knife, for skinning those squirrels and for that canoe I planned to build if we ran into a birch tree, but my knife was too long and clumsy to work a little thorn loose. All through the next day she whimpered, the limp more pronounced. When the leg itself began to swell, and she couldn't haul herself more than a few steps, we set up camp to wait for it to heal. If it healed. I wasn't so sure anymore that it was a thorn. We hid ourselves as best we could. June 25, by the tears in my hem.

The water was fifty feet across where we stopped. When Pete stepped in to try to scoop up a fish with his bare hands, I could see that the current ran strong. He waded in deeper and I held my heart in my hands, but the sight of that much water had us all giddy. Had he really seen a fish? Annie and I brought our rags down, waded in knee-deep after Pete, and scrubbed ourselves by twilight: it was early and dangerous to be moving about, but we couldn't resist showing off clean patches of skin. If we were shot, at least we'd go to watery graves. Ruby limped down to join us and snapped at the water, grabbing for minnows, but there were no minnows, and she only lapped up too much. I knew she'd be sick.

We'd been lucky with the weather, relatively speaking, but the next day, as we tried to sleep, the temperature spiked. Ruby made retching sounds. I pushed myself up on my elbows. Our shelters were low and never fully covered: we had plenty of downed trees, and the bugs to go with them, but not enough in the way of greenery. Ruby wriggled on her belly to get out.

Close to twilight again, long hours since we'd settled ourselves in. I peered outside and watched poor Ruby throw up a thin stream, then make loose hollow desperate sounds. Usually she turned to get permission before she left our campsites, but this time she wouldn't meet my eye. She bent her good knees and I thought she was going to settle herself down, but she got into crouching position and sprang. She wasn't hunting. She was like that dog watching for trucks, preparing to fling herself into the swift current below the bank where we camped. I wriggled out of the branches that made our door but she was already speeding down the bank toward the river, crippled and stumbling but relentless, gaining momentum. I strangled a cry and stretched out my arm as I ran—

* * *

That's where I always have to stop. Look, maybe you can kill off other people's dogs by suicide but it's no easy thing to kill your own. I can't let Ruby sacrifice herself so we can continue our journey, and I'm certainly not going to have her catch some magic fish that gives us the strength to carry on till we find the birch tree for our canoe and meet the wise Native American who guides us to freedom. Please.

I know, I know: everybody and his Hollywood uncle is telling a post-apocalyptic tale, but I'd like to point out that I haven't mentioned the apocalypse once, and I haven't put in zombies, either, though if you're looking for zombies, I'm here to tell you that they're living in the gated burbs of the once-great plains.

Maybe I'm just trolling for sympathy, putting my dog and my freckle-faced kids in the story. All right, I am trolling for sympathy. The truth is: Pete's just a babe in arms, his father's out till all hours to punish me, and Annie's not even hatched yet. Ruby's not exactly crippled, either. She's only as depressed as I am in this heat. I jabber at her as if she could speak my language, as if she could save me.

The women I know are lost to corporate lawyering and kitchen remodeling. About pregnancy I'm equal parts *Something to live for* and *How can I bring another child into this dying world.*

You start to think: those clowns have actually taken over. You start to think how the weather can't get any weirder, how somebody follows every keystroke, how nobody gets the joke. You start to think that Ruby knows something you don't know, because she looks like she does, she looks like she knows the secrets of the universe.

* * *

I stretch my arm out and now I'm running faster than Ruby, gaining on her. I can hear Pete running behind me, Annie behind him. Is it even right to stop her? Are we only prolonging her agony?

She enters the water and paddles with her three good legs. I fling myself after and when I reach her, it's not clear if I'm going to bring her down or she's going to bring me down. But I cling to her wet fur, as thick as the air in this godforsaken tornado-ridden Midwestern summer, as real to me as those children, swimming behind me into our future.

TIDAL WAVE

In THE EARLY DAYS OF integration, when only white girls tried out
for cheerleader, our elections were a cross between small-town participatory
democracy, Soviet-style anointment of the chosen, and the Miss America Pag-
eant. We sat rapt in the bleachers while the candidates cartwheeled in front
of the whole school, flashing their white panties. Then we trooped back to
homeroom to cast our votes.

We were chatterers, smarty-pants, A-track girls who raised our hands on
one beat and never let the boys get a word in edgewise. We would never be
cheerleaders, but we knew what it took: a cheerleader didn't need to be pretty,
though most of ours were pretty, as a matter of fact, and a cheerleader didn't
need to be athletic, though some of ours weren't too shabby in the handstand
department. A cheerleader only needed to exude unshakable self-confidence
and, maybe as a corollary, to beam bubbly friendliness and make it look like
it wasn't fake—we knew all about fake friendliness, we were growing up in
South Carolina, for God's sake.

All our stories are unresolved high school stories. We were the Tidal
Wave, the Class of '69 at Due East High School, our school years punctuated
by assassinations and riots, by the Tet Offensive, by flower children in San
Francisco whose very existence suggested that we were living in some remote
outpost of civilization that didn't get updates on a regular basis. The Due East
boys who couldn't get a word in edgewise volunteered to go to war while the
rest of America burned its draft cards. We heard that Bo Channing, who'd
just moved to Due East from Twentynine Palms, smoked pot, but we couldn't
imagine where he got hold of it or what would happen if the MPs caught him
with it on base. We couldn't imagine what we would do if Bo Channing cast
his icy-hot gaze on us.

We were a chorus that sang with one voice, and now in every Facebook post we hear one of those voices standing close. We spend all our waking hours online, poring over photos, but the only face we really care about seeing again is Vonda Freeman's. She was our Homecoming Queen, our Sweetheart of Due East High, and once upon a time we A-track girls were her court. She was—yes—our head cheerleader. She was also the most self-contained girl we ever knew, so we're not surprised she boycotts Facebook, but that doesn't stop us from looking for her night and day. That doesn't stop us from craving her love.

* * *

The minute we saw Vonda Freeman, in freshman year when she stepped off the bus from St. Elizabeth's Island, we were stunned by her eyes, a strange light green. Would she mesmerize the boys the way she mesmerized us? We weren't entirely sure she was beautiful, because redheads were not supposed to be beautiful, and the auburn brows framing her cat eyes drew too thick a line. She wasn't even tanned, which was a challenge to everything we knew about the attributes of beautiful girls. Mr. Thigsby said we were ignorant little yahoos, the way we slathered on baby oil and roasted ourselves at the beach, when for centuries poets had known the most beautiful skin was alabaster skin:

Look at Botticelli's Venus, look at Vonda Freeman, for goodness sake.

So we all did, we twisted in our seats toward the back of the room, where Vonda's face had turned one of those fiery shades that is certainly not alabaster. She wore an expression we had never seen on each other's faces, a combination of pain and shame and sweetness, and she stared down at her desk so assiduously that Mr. Thigsby said:

"Vonda sugar, I most certainly did not mean to put you on the spot, but now you have perfectly illustrated feminine grace."

Later, we all agreed that when she finally allowed herself to look up that day with her slow-breaking smile, her eyes darted toward Margaret Washington and Marcus Toomer, who stared out the window as assiduously as Vonda had stared down at her desk while the white folk discussed the perfect shade of pale.

* * *

We were a pod of porpoises swooping and diving through tidal creeks, and we had to have Vonda swimming among us. We worshipped Mr. Thigsby, but we resolved to take Vonda to the beach, to slather baby oil all down her white sloping back. We crammed in one car and headed to St. Elizabeth's, to the ends of the earth.

Bouncing down Vonda's dirt drive, lined with crushed shells, we remembered the oyster beds dying, the canning factory shuttered. The Freemans' yard was encased in chain link and covered by a tattered rug of brittle brown leaves. Beyond, their squat house was concrete block, its windows small enough for prison cells, because enlisted families always had to live like that. But the pines rose up like spires, the live oaks dangled dappled moss, the light was dreamlight. We smelled the marsh, somewhere close. Maybe the Freemans knew something we didn't know, something about what to do if the waters rose or the world came to its close.

A shadow passed the prison window and we exited the car as one pulsing heart. We knew that Vonda had brothers and sisters, six or seven, which meant they must be Catholic, our mothers said. It made us ashamed to look at Vonda's mother, who came to the door with a wan smile, her long thin hair a sickly yellow.

Our eyes trained above on a pileated woodpecker, rat-tat-tatting, mocking us. A preening bluebird perched below. Those birds never perched in our well-pruned trees. We never heard that low, clear hum.

* * *

We were bad as buzzards, scavengers, pickers at the dead meat of gossip. But what could we say about sweet Vonda? She looked like a candidate for all kinds of loving—hadn't Mr. Thigsby called her a goddess?—but her only dates were with Elliot Schwartzman, who was so far off in this math-and-science world that he and Herb, the Schwartzman twins, spoke a language nobody else understood. Yet somehow Elliott knew the words to ask her out and Vonda, for some reason nobody understood either, said yes.

One Wednesday night, cruising through town, we saw Vonda standing in front of the Church of God. Vonda, the Holy Rollers—did Elliott know about this? We turned our faces so she wouldn't see us gaping, but our screeches might have reached the moon. The church was asbestos shingle, raised off the ground, with big red doors the Rollers threw open when they got to rolling. We'd spent our whole lives staring at that church every time we drove by, hoping to see someone cavorting with the Spirit or shouting out in tongues, and sometimes we did see lumpy white folks pounding out the Jericho March, speaking a language stranger than the Schwartzman twins', a language that came from some place so far beyond Due East it was beyond our powers of imagination to conjure it. Our mothers said the way the Church of God carried on, they ought to call it *Church of the Holy Fools*.

Vonda could not possibly believe what Holy Rollers believed. When we craned our necks, we saw a scraggle of yellow hair swaying on the front steps, and Vonda yanking her mother so hard it looked as if she herself, our priestess, was on fire with the spirit.

Our screeching calmed. Would we tell? Or would we swallow her shame and make it our own?

* * *

A few years back, we heard her name on the radio: *Vonda Freeman-Toomer*. Within the hour, Mindy Bottom, who'd always claimed to be Vonda's closest friend, posted the NPR link. Our aging giggles rippled out across the Southeast as we played it again and again: Vonda at an Occupy demonstration in Oakland, our Vonda in California among the latter-day hippies. She said something sweet about idealistic young folks, and we pictured her casting her green eyes down. Then she led a chant into the people's mic and Mindy posted:

"She certainly is putting those old cheerleading skills to use."

We couldn't make out a word of her chant. Over and over, the segment came to a replayed end, till Mindy sent the link to Vonda's faculty page at Berkeley, where she taught physics: Vonda, a professor of quantum mechanics. We were tempted to email Herb Schwartzman, but we were too late: Elliott was already on the case, patiently instructing his Facebook friends in the mysteries of wave-particle duality and entangled twins.

Vonda was nothing like her mother and nothing like us: her hair was short, thick, pure white. We didn't know a single woman our age who even let the gray show. She wore old movie-star glasses, rhinestone-studded, and behind the lenses her eyes looked like they were lit up by the Due East sun. She was just starting on that slow-breaking smile, beautiful as ever.

* * *

Vonda's father was due to ship out to Vietnam, the way so many fathers did, but what could we do? We were the women's auxiliary, the U.S.O. girls. The war beamed at us day and night, from the *Today* Show and Walter Cronkite and even WAPE, the Big Ape out of Jacksonville, but we knew when to hold our tongues.

The Monday Vonda didn't get off the bus, Mindy Bottoms reported that she had seen the military police kick up white dust as they departed, speeding down the oyster-shell drive. Vonda's father hadn't shown up for the transport, so the MPs came to fetch him and when they got there—

He hid from them *under the bed*.

We gaped. According to Mindy, Sgt. Freeman didn't want blood on his hands. After they took him away, Vonda locked herself in her room, which as we all knew wasn't a room at all but a large closet, and wouldn't answer a knock except to say:

"Mindy, you are my closest friend but I don't know that I'll ever come out."

The truth was, Vonda wasn't anybody's closest friend: she was our porcelain doll, and we fussed over her, but did any of us ever get close? We imagined her on her knees, losing track of day and night, mumbling strange Holy Rollers syllables no one could understand. After he heard the story, Elliott Schwartzman yanked his curls and paced the lunchroom. He stopped in front of our table to keen:

"What if they handcuffed him?"

We had not pictured that, but now we did, and more: what if they shackled him and took him to Vietnam a prisoner in chains? A father who didn't do his duty shook us like nothing our parents had ever done, not tomcatting fathers or mothers with sherry-breath. Mindy's mother had swallowed all her sleeping pills once, but this was different: this was shoving your finger in the whole country's eye. Hiding under the bed, drunk or sober, wasn't something we would call manly.

The longer Vonda stayed away from school, the more we shivered at the memory of the down on her cheek when the light dappled through the moss. We pictured Vonda's father smoking pot and dressed in women's underwear. Where had we picked up such notions? He could get killed in Vietnam!

We even said it aloud. Not a month after Vonda came back to school, they called her to the office to get the news. When she walked back into A-track trig, the sight of her was hard to take in: Mr. Thigsby said beauty required a flaw, but surely he didn't mean a glob of snot stuck to her upper lip. She didn't look beautiful—she didn't even look pretty—but she did look like someone who would mow us all down if she said so much as a word. The student teacher stood slack-jawed, helpless, while the rest of us stared down at our desks assiduously, which Vonda had taught us to do. She gathered up her things.

Vonda's father, who hadn't wanted to go to war, who'd done something you just didn't do, was dead, dead, dead. Now everything was wrong, upside down and inside out, every truth we'd ever breathed in with the salt air that blew through these islands. If there was a God, why did he make Vonda for such suffering? Oh God, why did you make us for such suffering? We couldn't find out about the funeral: no one knew, not even Elliott Schwartzman. We called and we called, but not one of the Freeman children ever picked up the phone. Our mothers said:

"Stop calling, why don't you. They've gone to bury whatever's left of him."

We snuck our extensions into our closets. We were as bad as B-track boys who knew they were going to get turned down but had to keep asking for the date. She was the most elusive girl at Due East High School and we knew we couldn't have her but we just couldn't stop.

* * *

Vonda's father dying turned the very tide. When she came back to school, Elliott had already lost her to her grief. She walked dazed and unearthly through the halls, and Mr. Thigsby whispered "Ophelia" when she passed. The whole football team tripped over each other to save her from other boys on the team who might take advantage of her sorrow, and she latched onto a halfback as her protector. We heard that Vonda Freeman put out for her halfback, because that was what boys said about girls. It wasn't enough, though, not in that place, not in that time. Soon enough we heard that Vonda put out for Marcus Toomer too.

Marcus Toomer. *Miscegenation* was a word our teachers hissed, as if the very concept were obscene. In the spring of '68, the spring Martin Luther King was killed, it did not matter that Mr. Thigsby had marched for voting rights. Marcus and Vonda could have been killed too.

Our mothers said they were asking for trouble, letting Marcus run for Student Council president. The three candidates sat in folding chairs on the gym floor in front of the stage and we sat before them, docile lambs craving a shepherd. One by one they went to the podium to deliver their speeches. First

Calhoun Booth stumbled and forgot the jokes he'd practiced. We remember Herb Schwartzman next, droning on while Elliott, his campaign manager, mouthed the whole boring speech in unison from high in the bleachers.

Marcus sat in his folding chair with some of that self-possession we'd seen in Vonda, as if he knew perfectly well that it was his turn to speak but declined the opportunity, thank you kindly. Then the curtains on the stage above parted to reveal a band: two hulking guitarists, a sleepy-eyed drummer, a bassist with an Angela-Davis Afro. We'd never seen such a thing on such a day. We'd certainly never seen a girl bassist. Marcus had enlisted the officers' sons with the longest hair, the hair they grew to spite their father's High and Tights: that was Bo Channing on drums, probably stoned out of his mind. The band struck a chord, and we all swallowed little strangled cries when they launched into a soul version of "Revolution."

That song acted as a drug on us: we were bedazzled, ecstatic, released. Bo Channing slurred the words but we didn't need the words. We saw Vonda's mother swaying outside the church, Vonda kneeling by the bedside where her father was rolled up like a rug, hiding from the military police. His hand reached out to grab her white leg and then—poof, presto-change-o—the song was over. The assistant principal pulled the switch to draw the curtains and Marcus Toomer walked to the podium, the slightest smile playing on his lips.

We tensed as the band marched down the side stage steps (remember, this was the spring of James Earl Ray). Marcus reached the microphone and nonchalantly spoke a line we'd only heard on Walter Cronkite:

"Power to the people."

Bo Channing, halfway down the steps, raised a drumstick high, and the gymnatorium erupted. From that moment, we knew Marcus would pull it off. We ached for whatever he could see so clearly. We were his acolytes now, in our bleacher row, his fan club, his groupies. We felt Vonda's body heat radiating. Who was to say that Mr. Thigsby wasn't right? Who was to say our churches weren't crazy too, blessing fighter jets?

It was as if she could hear my thoughts: Vonda looked at me—not at us, at me. It was the longest gaze anyone had ever directed my way, her smile full-throttle for once. We were alone. I was alone. My eyes locked with hers. She knew the thoughts I thought. She knew who'd called and called. She knew I loved her, and now I loved Marcus too, and I didn't even know what I meant by *love*. She knew I'd never speak my thoughts, not now, not on Facebook, not ever.

* * *

After the NPR story, that picture of Vonda adorned a dozen Facebook walls. Did Marcus shoot it? There was no Marcus Toomer we could positively ID as our Marcus in the first twelve Google pages, though both the pastor and the political consultant looked like possibilities. Mindy tweeted them out into the void.

For weeks, we played the interview. We could make out the words by then: Vonda was chanting "Power to the people," of course. It echoed down the mic line, enough to make us want to drive downtown in the middle of the night to occupy Atlanta and Charleston and Charlotte. But we were not the occupying sort, so we occupied Facebook instead. While we were trying to locate Marcus, scanned black-and-white snapshots from the Tidal Wave days crowded the walls: Marcus under-exposed, Vonda too pale and perfect to keep onscreen for long. She made our eyes sting.

Our nostalgia weighed down the Cloud, and eventually the others moved on, even Mindy. Grandchildren replaced the old high school pictures just as the Occupy tents started to disappear, like that tide: turning, then turning back.

* * *

For a brief while we were upstarts. We stuck our fingers in our parents' eyes and voted for Marcus Toomer: he was Marvin Gaye and we were his back-up singers. We said things we'd never dreamed of saying—*Keep the faith, baby, fight the power*—but the rumors were carpet bombs, exploding all around us. Vonda never told us she was seeing Marcus. She told us she was going out for cheerleader.

"For cheerleader," we repeated, uncomprehending as our mothers.

The concrete-block house and the dead father and the Holy Rollers? And now Marcus? We even thought, for one split second, that she might not win—the gossip was sticky as napalm, adhering to her perfect skin—but Vonda did fine at the audition. What could we say about whooping and shaking a pompom? Everyone she'd been kind to voted for her, and of course all the boys who were mesmerized, and we voted for her too. We were loyal, we were faithful, and that was that. Vonda was an actual cheerleader: our friend Vonda Freeman.

Of course the other cheerleaders took her under their shapely wings, whereas we were just boring A-track girls, some of us a little plump. The cheerleaders were certainly super-friendly. Vonda never acted like she was too good for us. She never let on what she knew about me, and I never let on what I knew about her. And maybe we were both wrong. Maybe I didn't love her, and maybe she didn't disappear into the ranks of the girls beaming self-confidence to protect him, to protect them both.

Even before Facebook, we thought of her over the years. Mr. Thigsby was wrong about the flaw: we never saw Vonda's. But when the assistant principal announced the scholarships, we didn't know why Vonda would want to go to hoity-toity Bryn Mawr, so far away. And "Marcus Toomer, Haverford"—we'd never heard of Haverford. What was a pair of Quaker schools, or geography for that matter, to the Tidal Wave? We heard that they were married and year after year we looked for them at our reunions. We had three interracial couples by our twentieth, and by the thirtieth we wouldn't have been surprised to see somebody walk in with a gay partner—though they haven't, not yet. Vonda and Marcus could certainly have come to a reunion, but they never did. They never came.

* * *

With husband number three, I moved to the Atlanta burbs like everybody else, but I miss the lowcountry like a limb that's been taken from me. "The prelapsarian beauty," as Mr. Thigsby used to call it, the dirty-lace look of Spanish moss hanging from live oaks in Vonda Freeman's chain-linked yard. Vonda was right about one thing: I don't tell people in Smyrna what I'm thinking. I can't picture myself at a demonstration. I can't imagine.

After the Charleston shootings, Facebook pop-pop-pops with the Rebel flag. Every few days, a new firefight breaks out and the ghost of Mr. Thigsby weeps. I find myself staring into another void. I open Vonda Freeman's faculty page and gaze again into her light eyes. Vonda gazes back, zapped by the miracle of quantum-something-or-other into my condo. I could reach out and touch her face.

I do reach out. I stretch a hand toward the wavering screen. We're in the Holy Rollers Church. All around us, Rollers sway and moan while we sit silent, side by side. The air's charged, as if a hurricane's about to swoop in, and outside the birds chatter, sly prophets planning where to meet after the waters rise. I feel Vonda's body warm against mine. It takes me a while to see that the preacher standing in front of us is Marcus, grown portly. They both know something I don't know. When Marcus summons me to rise, I realize I can translate that one line he keeps chanting.

"Right on," I whisper, but no sound comes out. Marcus doesn't hear me. He doesn't see me, either.

I'm not there.

I'm not anywhere, and Vonda has marched off into the night without me. I hear birds chattering still, though the dark stretches deep. The screen pulses on, looking assiduously for its absent Facebook queen.

CHILDREN OF NIGHT

Francis, blind, blesses his blindness. Francis, blind, blesses. . . .

THE MANTRA STREAMS FOR HOURS, seeping from some deep cavern of my brain. A poem? A song? Definitely from the peace-and-love days—sounds like Leonard Cohen or one of those flowers-in-her-hair folkies—but I can't summon a tune and without wristies or chips there's no way to check the source.

"Why are you holding your head?" Andy signs from his corner of the garage, because it's dusk outside and people might already be about. When daylight comes again, we'll throw caution to the non-existent winds and whisper. We've kept the old hours since before we went into hiding, but the rest of the country obeys the mandatory reversal and, in daylight, goes inside to sleep—if they can, since Climate Control locked the air systems. The old garage, of course, has no air system whatsoever and reaches hellish heat by mid-day. If not for the ancient oak drooping over our roof, we would have shriveled.

"I don't know," I sign back, though I know perfectly well. I'm holding my head because I have no other way to contain my rage at Francis for reminding me of blindness. When I was young and romantic and religious, I actually routed prayers through Francis, the sentimental-favorite saint, the tree-and-animal-hugger saint, the easy saint. All that—belief, prayer, Francis—was long ago, yet this very morning, Andy said I'd cried out prayers in my sleep.

"Wouldn't that be rich?" he whispered, not unkindly, as dawn was breaking. "If we were betrayed by your involuntary prayers?" His little fugitive joke.

* * *

Noreen comes at high noon with three days' meals disguised in a thick standard-issue garbage bag. It's risky: noon is the new midnight, but neighbors could still look out their windows to wonder why she's emptying her trash at that ungodly hour. She wears a huge sunhat and eyeshields, so when the old deadbolt slides open and she slips the bag in the waiting can, we see mostly bobbing hat. She's begged us not to blow kisses or wave, not to acknowledge her in any way, so we avert our eyes, good parents disappearing into the seams of the garage. Tonight, if I've counted right, is her licensed provisions night, so we'll have a longer look at her in only twelve hours, when she comes to the garage to get the Wiggy and drive off

After she leaves, Andy and I inch toward the food from our corners, prizefighters approaching worthy opponents. At the barred windows, we duck creakily: even in the dark interior we might be detected. Foot patrols scan the alleys three or four times a week in daylight, less at night when everyone's out and about and doing their dirty work. In the dark, children instructed to be on the lookout for fugitives sometimes peer in. It won't help to tell a spying child that we're just a couple of geezer wise guys who said the wrong thing to a Constitutional Guard.

That is, I said the wrong thing to a Constitutional Guard.

Andy always reaches the food bin first and doesn't seem to know I let him win. He raises his fists—the champ—and dances a restrained victory-jig. That's how I know we're going to get out of here. It may be the last sign of hope I see for the next three days, so I savor it. It's all I can do not to lay a hand to his when I reach him, but I know that my touch would be as creepy as a black widow's to him now.

He doles out the water reluctantly, as if he's afraid I'll take more than my three jars. Have I been that grabby during our life together? I marvel again at the weight Noreen must surreptitiously haul across the yard to keep us alive. The first week, she sent cheese-laden palm leaves, succulent with the caramelized carrots she bought on the black vegetable market for my eyes. The plan was for us to eat a home-cooked meal the first day, then subsist on little cans of farmed herring and xerophyte chips—but you try forcing down food that tastes like old tires in an airless garage. We left the cans unopened. Now she sends us green bananas from the Ohio groves and coconut bars coated in local chocolate. We've become our daughter's children, grabbing up the sweets and gobbling them first.

She promised she'd put a red napkin in the food-pack if anything changed, if we should hold out hope for a miraculous removal of our names from the Fugitive List, so Andy shakes the empty bag upside down as he always does, looking for the sign. Both of us know no red napkin will flutter to the concrete garage floor, only Simon and Noreen's old unitunes, meant to be our change of clothes. We go commando underneath. My tunic's hot pink, sleeveless, and low-cut, a sorrow on a woman my age. Over my left breast—or where my left breast stood twenty years ago—the logo says "TECHNOL-OGY RULES." On the back it says "Nuclear is forever."

I'm glad I'll never see my sorry reflection in this shirt, not that I trust my own vision. I was scheduled for the flash cataract removal the week we went into hiding and now, as the months pass, everything grows indistinct. I fret that it's more than cataracts making my vision fuzzy, that I've succumbed to the retinopathy that blinded my mother. Andy and I are both covered with arthritic knobs and cysts. Our ears ring, our hearts race, our hands tremble. Our bodies smell so rank we've lost the sense of smell. Andy's beard has grown biblical, though there are still bald patches on his cheeks, so he's a comic prophet. I should talk: wiry whiskers sprout from my chin. Wild-eyed elders, we'll be relegated to the Permanently Disabled List and sent to live in auto-mated care centers, where my world will dim to darkness and strange phrases will pop into my head to torment me. I grab up my supplies and retreat to my corner, that line playing on an endless loop. *Francis, blind. . . .*

What sort of fugitive am I, living in a two-car garage, that old temple of middle-class respectability? That first night we arrived safely, Simon sneered: "You're not exactly Anne Frank, you know. This is not the Underground Railroad."

* * *

I think I hear wind, though it's only March and the windstorms don't usually start till April now. Everything comes earlier or later, so I never adjust, and I've completely lost track of the passing months. All February I knelt by the door, even on these knees, to catch the scent of roses. "Smell the roses!" I whispered to Andy, another little fugitive joke. Noreen has somehow managed to save one bush, maybe the last rosebush in the Midwest. Until she got enough cacti for camouflage, her neighbors accused her of hoarding water—little do they know how much she's hoarding now. We can't afford to wonder how she man-ages. Today may be the day we come up with a plan to escape, to stop putting her at risk. Today may be the day the insurrection throws everything into a chaos that will cloak us. We've heard more sirens lately, though God knows our imaginations trick us.

Of course we know the garage by heart: would that there were more to know. Brick walls—another reason we've made it this long, that and the slate roof—and handsome oak rafters inside, refurbished elegantly like the rest of Noreen and Simon's tasteful landmark house. Nothing hangs from those rafters. No worktable like Andy's, cluttered with tools and gadgets, rests against the walls. An antique sled—the children can't fathom what it's for, no matter how many times their parents explain—hangs on the wall alongside one expensive rake and one expensive hoe, those too unused, but Noreen's a multivalent quantum engineer who values tools. A forty-pound bag of cactus food: that just slays us. And of course the Wiggy. Only the most expensive model for Noreen and Simon, regulation neon yellow, on my side of the garage. As I inch along the wall I trace the curve of its roof, the cliff that drops behind two little seats, the tiny tires, the tightly-folded wings: it's a clown-car, but I can make out its shape without panicking again about impending blindness, and so I feel affection. Once we all thought these gliders would save us, but the Wiggys—like the eyeshields, like Climate Control—came too late.

When we first moved in at Christmastime, we thought the Wiggy was our magical carriage. We planned to sleep upright behind its tinted glass, but it's torture to bend our old backs into the mini-seats and anyway, we might expire from the stench. Andy's rigged up porta-potties for us, clever stands he made from the neat bundles of ancient garden stakes. We insert a dusty little magicello garden bag and, when we can squeeze anything out, tie it up immediately—sometimes tough dogs that have survived the ban roam the neighborhood, sniffing. Even the dogs, fellow fugitives, would betray us. Day or night, we crawl over to put the bag behind the Wiggy's seats. On her shopping trip Noreen will glide our waste wherever she takes it, another dangerous act. I can't bear to think about how she manages that either.

I really can't fathom why we don't just lie down in the dust to die, but we curl up instead on bamboo yoga mats we found rolled on the shelf. I see Andy holding his head now, and I make the same "Why-are-you-holding-your-head" sign he made to me. He points directly to his partially-completed implant site, *partially* another stroke of luck that's kept us alive and free. We were the last holdouts, though Simon and Noreen swore there was nothing to fear from the Gibson chips: they were such a convenience. The chip would see for me if my vision went! But blind or sighted, I want my own organic brain to be the only witness to my secrets and sins. For a while it looked as if Andy would be my partner in paranoia, but he's always been a sucker for gizmos.

At least at his age he had to wait to check for rejection before the chip went live. On the trip home from the insertion, I prayed that sometime in the waiting period he'd change his mind. I didn't like the way he looked, head bent forward, stunned from the implant. Because we still drove our old pavement-only solar see-through, we were already the object of attention, and a CG on foot patrol waved me over. The guard trotted up but kept his distance, clicked his palm amplification button, barked that he'd just seen my vehicle two hours before. I hollered my responses through the open window. I told him about our special permit, but I was flustered as always before authority and searched a little wildly through the handheld for the license. I wasn't used to driving in the middle of the night, wasn't used to the reverse hours everyone else kept, wasn't used to being so frightened.

The CG pointed to my handheld—probably he'd never seen one so old, and maybe he'd never seen one at all. Under his visor-light I thought I could see beads of shiny terror forming on his own thin upper lip. "Drop that!" He thought I had an explosive.

"Don't be a knucklehead," I called. It just popped out, the same silly phrase I directed at Noreen when she told us she was marrying Simon, the most ridiculous thing I could have said to a daughter who promptly ran straight into the arms of the man who'd agreed to marry her without her data. Now I'd said it to a CG who held my freedom in his hands.

Even in the nightlight I could see veins bursting on the guard's ruddy face. He was a kid, the kind of self-important, marble-white kid they recruit for the hot boredom of night foot patrol. He tapped his blue-veined forehead, his own knucklehead, to make a transmission. "Bringing in two OWOs," he told whoever listened at the other end, but I was still not used to autophone. Even I knew the CG's acronym for old folks, but Andy and I weren't On the Way Out. I liked to think we were generously middle-aged. I still scrolled recklessly, searching for the license.

Beside me, Andy muttered, "Gun it." I thought he was hallucinating from the brain-stun, but gradually it dawned on me: Andy was telling me to gun it because he thought we'd never get out of an interrogation without being subjected to some kind of torture session, even once they'd located our license, even if we were On the Way Out. I'd dissed a Constitutional Guard. They would scan our files and discover open-channel comments we'd sent after too much palm wine.

It's not as if you have time for rational thought at a time like that. By then, I'd gunned it and jettisoned the handheld out the open window. As air roared in from the blast furnace outside, Andy lifted his head to direct me down back alleys. He knew more about CG facilities than any of us—before we went into hiding, he was a defense lawyer who heard the worst interrogation stories—so for once I did as he said.

Big screens haven't been around for years, but that day, as I raced the solar to the outskirts of Greenglass, I starred in a 2-D big-budget Hollywood production. We ditched the car, then huffed and puffed a mile into an abandoned barn that reminded us of our past. If we'd had any sense of decency, any impulse to save our daughter the danger we now cause her, we would have politely dehydrated in that hayloft. But no. Living beings cling to life. For a few days we survived on old scraps of spilled animal feed and rancid rainwater pooled in rusty cans. Andy tasted rock-hard dung—we were desperate—and spat it out. Finally, another stroke of good fortune: one of the western volcanoes erupted yet again, and in the dark spew of her ash drifting eastward we were able to scurry in daylight from alley to alley, stealing fistfuls of water from the winter barrels. The theft of even a handful would have given a CG permission to shoot us on sight, but we were in a part of the city that's short on CGs and ashy with or without volcanoes. The dark-skinned poor inhabit those streets, half their young men zapped in the frontal lobes. It's our version of lobotomies: everything old is new again, even in end times. We were spotted, I'm sure we were, but nobody turned us in—with your frontal lobes out of commission, it must be hard to summon the energy.

Finally we moved through more prosperous zones, too exhausted to appreciate the irony of the wealthy in the inner city, and wept when we finally saw the sign:

The Personal Responsibility = Personal Wealth Authority Welcomes You to Old Town: A Healthy Individuation Community.

We dragged our haggard, dehydrated, individuated selves to Noreen and Simon's stately pickled house under cover of ash. At the back door, Simon's jaw snapped like a pit bull's under his thick red beard while he pretended not to know us, but Noreen yanked the door open wide enough for us to crawl through.

The CGs had no way to link us to our daughter: Noreen's records were lost when one of the early floods destroyed a primitive data center. No one would come round to question her, not in this part of town, and we thought we could hide in their basement and bide our time reading—Noreen's our child, data or no data, with enough spirit to keep a box of the old texts hidden away in a dark recess. But Simon was sure our grandchildren would spot us, and reminded us that it wouldn't be fair or even sane to expect them to keep such a secret. *You're not runaway slaves.*

I admit I haven't been a good grandmother to the triplets: all three girls are a little remote, a little superior to our strange old-fashioned ways. I'm jealous of the way they took Noreen from us so completely, how they finished that job that Simon started. I can't always tell one triplet from the other. I can't follow the games they tap on their foreheads.

What could we do? We skulked off to the garage. Once we rehydrated, we'd think of a plan—but we have no plan, no more ash to hide our flight. We considered stealing the Wiggy, but we don't know how to glide and even now, we're not desperate enough to betray Noreen.

* * *

The wind picks up—I haven't imagined it. Anticipation seeps in through the cracks. Andy does jumping jacks against the wall, which alarms me: his flapping arms might attract a day patrol. Does he think he's urging the wind along? He hasn't tried that kind of exercise in weeks, and I've very nearly given up any movement beyond racing him to the porta-potty. It's desperately hard to not-think of water. Thinking will lead me to empty the three jars prematurely, and I mustn't do that if I want to live. Do I want to live? Every joint stings, humiliated like the rest of me.

If it weren't so dangerous to summon memory, I could distract myself by turning the past, too, into a Hollywood production. But it is dangerous. Not-thinking about our past's as hard as not-thinking about water. I wince at Andy, touching his toes now, looking ridiculous, a tattered tunic on a stick. The new unitune he's taken from the food bag has big block letters that might say "Get real" or "Gee whiz" or "God damn." Strange shadows have fallen on our concrete floor. The hot wind outside stokes my old fury and I can't stop the scenes of our youth from flashing.

Who needs a Gibson chip? I see those days bright and clear: the old dove-gray farmhouse, the sagging barn, the struggling crops. We spent the early days of our marriage in an idyll, Children of Light, "an intentional community," our mimeographed newsletter said. "Seems more unintentional to me," Andy used to say. We knew less than nothing. We were hippies with a spiritual bent and we thought we were frolicking through paradise. Everyone at Children of Light agreed on faith, but faith in what, exactly, was not entirely clear. We crowded into the kitchen at all hours of day and night to out-sanctify each other and got each other hot instead.

If we wanted privacy, Andy and I lay up high on the rude planks of the barn loft, where touching each other on a summer afternoon left us slick as seals. The goats wandered between barn and farmyard, devouring everything in their path, and we called them the way we imagined Francis would have: "Sister Goat, please don't eat those work gloves." The gloves were long gone. When we drank her thick warm milk for the first time, we gagged. Poor Sister Goat. We killed her unintentionally, the way we killed the chickens, and the kale and the spinach yellowing even then in the angry sun. The turnips and potatoes lay desiccated under the earth, its core already bubbling upward to destroy us. None of us at Children of Light knew the least thing about farming. Andy used to say God sent the intelligent life to other planets and gave earth the know-nothings. As the crops and animals failed, Children of Light descended into breast-beating piety and forced cheerfulness, and I knew my fellow communards were shedding their faith like winter fur. I felt my own falling off.

I watched Andy fall in love with one of the singles. I'd been cranky, I admit—you try living with a bunch of religious nuts—so my handsome young husband picked a paragon of patience. I suppose her long skirts and long sleeves were meant to signify her modesty in an age of sexual license. I could sense him mooning over her golden braids as she stood at the sink, washing our dishes, cleaning our mess, no self-sacrifice too large for her sunny saintliness. Her name was Mary: of course. She wove flowers into those braids—that made me gag, too—and when it was her turn to lead us in hippie-dippie prayers, I had to leave the table. There. That was it. I rewind blessings-at-table and hear her chirp: "Francis, blind, blesses his blindness."

My turn to windmill my arms. Andy thinks he can summon a storm? I wish the hot air outside would knock these brick walls down. My arms beat out the rhythm of St. Mary's mantra: "Francis, blind. Francis, blind. Francis, blind." I might burst with venom. And that, of course, was exactly how I felt near the end at Children of Light. The hotter I burned, the more Andy drifted into Mary's cool orbit. Finally, one sweltering August night, I heard the two them creep out for some assignation: an innocent walk-and-talk, I imagined, but still it enraged me. I fled in the commune's old pick-up to my mother's house in town, where I sobbed the whole betrayal story.

"You should have some faith in him," my mother said mildly. And then, as if it weren't completely contradictory: "Even if he did take up with her, he's very young. You'll just have to forgive him."

When Andy hitchhiked after me, and I asked if he'd fallen in love with Mary, he said: "Not intentionally." A little Children of Light joke. His look was so strange I didn't know if it signaled his innocence or guilt, but I knew how to read the silence that followed. Forgive that.

Somehow we got past it: I don't know if you call that forgiveness. As the years passed and the earth heated, belief itself seemed more and more childish, false innocence in a dangerous age. When Noreen began to study quantum mechanics, and delighted in parallel universes, I soaked it up with her. How could I believe in God after the God-particle, the Trinity after triad-beams? What sort of God would create a lush earth only to fry it? Andy ignored my revenge dalliances, and I ignored his moral superiority, but eventually even he refused to belong to an institution whose clergy out-authoritarianed the Constitutional Guard.

Another memory flickers: chandelier light. Andy and Simon in the elegant dining room around Noreen's big oak table. Sunday dinner with the aged parents. Bored out of their wits by our conversation, the little girls tapped their foreheads surreptitiously, watching flickies, and Andy tapped his forehead too, not realizing he was mimicking the children, trying to contain his frustration. "Don't you get the joke, Simon? Protecting liberty by taking it away?" Simon stared out, another creepy habit. His gray eyes never made contact: no wonder he didn't recognize us at his door. That Sunday he was expressing mild sympathy for the Guards, for putting up with arrogant Old Towners, for keeping his daughters safe from the shadowy figures who make their way into even his fortified sub-city. He had a piece of packaged protein stuck between his teeth, or anyway I put a piece of protein there when I picture him. I watch Simon, too spineless to argue his point, rise to land a big sloppy protein-laden kiss on the top of Noreen's head. That showy gesture, too, repels me.

The real torment of this garage is that I live too much in the past. I drift until I realize that Andy's waving his arm across the room, this time to get my attention. "Listen," he signs. I hear the old oak tree creak above us. Andy's eyes flash at the prospect of an out-of-season storm; as if in answer the sky slits itself open and spills down hail. Hail! We haven't seen such a thing in years, and hearing it ricochet off the slate is almost as good as seeing it. Thunderbooms rattle us, and I watch Andy slide down to his knees in thanksgiving for water in any form.

The temperature drops by the minute. I'm giddy with joy, my bitterness swept away, as lightning rips through Noreen's cactus garden. I'll bet the little girls are crowded at the window—I can't tell, in the storm, if it's day or night anymore, if my grandchildren are asleep or awake, but I have the strangest urge to pick them up to the glass and tell them how hailstorms used to form. How they form this very instant.

We feel the great shudder, the old oak riven when lightning strikes above. The splintered branch, stubborn as the rest of that death-defying tree, hesitates coming down. Its weight could flatten us when it finally descends, but we sit there grinning like clowns—at least I do. I can't make Andy out at all in the dimming light, so when he reaches me—he's crawled across the garage—I let out a little yelp of surprise. The fury outside drowns the sound, and Andy throws his body over mine (a little melodramatically, a little cinematically) to shield me from the thick creaking branch that will land any minute, bringing the roof down with it. I haven't felt his dry skin in so long I think at first that I'm touching tree bark. We wait and we wait. We wait so long that Andy must finally peel his arthritic self off. I'm touched by the chivalry, but it's a relief when he hoists his overripe body up. I haven't lost my sense of smell after all.

The instant Andy rises, the big branch breaches the roof, glances off, crashes onto the cacti. We rush to the hole above, liquid rushing down, both of us opening our mouths like newborn birds. It's not hail but warm water now, thick with organic matter. We gulp down all we can, so greedy we don't even hear at first the desperate jiggling of the door. Noreen, who always punches the code so precisely, so discreetly from her chip, can't get in.

Andy opens the deadbolt the old-fashioned way and we freeze when the door swings open: it's Simon on the threshold. I can hardly make him out, much less recognize him, but I see his beard soaked into a burlesque mask. "Get into the Wiggy," he chokes, so urgent that I almost forget this man is sympathetic to the Guards. I move toward the glider, but Andy holds me back.

"What's the plan?" Andy begins a lawyerly interrogation, the two men hissing at each other in the clattering rain, the door not even properly locked behind them. I can't hear any better than I can see. I stand beneath the newly-rent hole in the roof and try to make out the gash in the tree, the open wound. Beyond, a green sky pocked with scarlet cloud pustules descends. It must be twilight, or stormlight, or maybe it really is end times. We shouldn't have joked about that.

Simon, a desperado heading off the posse, looks straight into Andy's eyes as he argues, and I hear shards of his answer: "Resisters. . .provisions." Maybe those are the syllables I want to hear. He turns to me again and barks: "Fold yourself up behind the seats." He means atop our waste bags. I've never heard him so resolute before. Has Noreen come up with a plan? The black market's one thing, but resisters are quite another, and Simon could well be delivering us to the guards. I have never trusted this man Noreen trusts.

"Noreen," I whimper, but he shoos me toward the Wiggy. "The girls."

"Safe, safe inside. Go. Go!"

Every resentment I've ever felt—at Andy for cheating, at Simon for being Simon—surges through my body. How many fugitives have prayed for deliverance, only to be delivered to the enemy? Wouldn't that be rich, if I must have faith in Simon to leave this prison, and then must forgive him at another prison's door?

Andy makes his wager and stands by the passenger door, waiting for me to join him. I'm not sure I can trust anyone's judgment, after all these months of hiding, but I climb into the back of the Wiggy and stretch myself face-down over the bags of our excrement. Liquid seeps onto the overhang of my hands, and I gag. Inter urinas et faeces nascimur. Already I'm twisted into a torture position. I've lost track of day and night, light and dark, and I know now that I'm losing my sight even faster than I feared. At least I've stopped gagging. I remember incongruously how much I loved gliding when Noreen first treated me to a ride.

Simon backs up the Wiggy, moves forward, accelerates. I feel the wings unfold. We rise, and in the thrill of flight I forget that we are geezers on the lam. I let myself imagine that wherever Simon is driving us, prison or refuge, the low green sky will eventually lift too. Maybe, from some slit of window, I'll catch dim sight of the cool moon, the stars I haven't seen for so long, the distant planets bursting with intelligent life.

SLEEPWALK

Maybe the whole thing could be accounted for by those times: how we—well, I—woke at three in the morning with a funny sensation that something, somebody, was missing, and wandered out to the living room where my childhood sweetheart, the love-of-my-life Richie, was supposed to be sleeping on the couch. He was gone. He hadn't even shut the door all the way. I leaned out the front window and caught sight of him crossing Broadway between 106th and 107th, jaywalking behind a *Daily News* delivery truck in his bare feet. He was naked except for his underwear, white huggies with holes in back I could see even from six flights up.

Thank God it was spring: a warm spring, almost a year since Kent State and nine months since the draft lottery for guys born in 1951. Richie was number 37, which meant he had to either stay in school or ship out to Vietnam, but he'd got himself tangled up in some Weathermen business. Now he was on the lam—or so he had told us a few hours before, over a bowl of chili. It was hard to say exactly how much beer we'd drunk at that point: he and Jean-Paul kept popping up to go buy another bottle of Miller High Life, the pair of them insisting *No man it's on me.* Mainly they wanted to put some distance between each other. All guys were like that, I thought then, like the city dogs you'd see on the sidewalk or in Riverside Park, shepherds and huskies on little leather leads, their owners holding them back when another dog passed and hissing, "Is he male? Is he male? Cause if he's male . . ."

If he's male, my dog'll go for blood and here's fair warning. Well, we had no warning from Richie. He just rang the buzzer downstairs and the next thing I knew he was at the apartment door, the two of us hugging and bawling. Jean-Paul wasn't home yet and Richie bent his knees to get down to my height and rub up against me the way he used to do when we were fourteen and fifteen and sixteen. I half-wanted him to make all the other moves too, the tongue in my mouth and the one-handed breast squeeze, but he didn't, he just held on for dear lustful life.

"Twenty years old, Feeney? Frigging married? Where's the little tyke?"

"That's not the only reason people get married." With his breath on my neck, though, I couldn't remember what the other reasons were. Jean-Paul and I had been planning to move in together but my father had lung cancer in a bad way and my mother said she'd slam the door in my face if I showed up, unwed and cohabitating, to visit him. So while the rest of the world cavorted in communes, here we were in a minuscule claustrophobic apartment, lawfully wed.

And here was Richie, his hair tied back with a shoelace and his sleeves rolled to his elbows. Over the fifth or sixth quart of beer he asked Jean-Paul—not me—if he could crash: "We got a safe house lined up in Brooklyn. Park Slope, man, a duplex this chick is renting for us, only the owner's sniffing around. Two days, maybe three? I'd really appreciate it."

"Must be weird to be back in New York," Jean-Paul said, non-committal. He didn't like the Weather Underground and he didn't like the idea of the feds showing up at our door.

"Dig it. But I couldn't stay in Madison with this shit going down. Cozy in my safe little school with Kissinger napalming every country in southeast Asia?" Richie wasn't the least concerned about insulting those of us who'd stayed in our safe little schools. We still didn't know exactly what he'd done, but when I leaned in to ask, Jean-Paul signaled with his eyebrows to keep still: the less we knew the better. He was probably right.

"Just don't go blowing anybody up." I pictured the front page of the *News* when they blew up that townhouse in the Village: a nail bomb, and three of them dead. *Rich kids,* Jean-Paul said.

Richie could be pretty reckless, but now he gave me his Agony in the Garden look. "We look at every action from every angle, man. I guess there's not a lotta politics in a theater department."

"There's enough." The truth was, Jean-Paul was the most political guy I knew, but he was full of contempt for the hotheads who said they were going out to smash up the Bank of America: the Richies. *You watch*, he always said. *They'll be working for the Bank of America ten years from now.*

"We've been doing some good street theater." Even to me it sounded like my little-girl voice.

"Oh wow," Richie snorted. "Street theater."

Jean-Paul was glowering by then. Richie was a ballplayer—a pitcher, tall and muscular—and he was a talker, a snorter, a stand-up guy who'd just walked away from his Wisconsin scholarship to get messed up in whatever he was messed up in. He didn't have a lot of patience for the Jean-Pauls of the world and the Jean-Pauls—the ones who went on the marches but wouldn't smash the windows—always looked like they were trying to figure out if they could take him down. The answer was: no. Jean-Paul was dark and intense and good-looking, the lead in the last three mainstage productions, but his hair was cut short for *Waiting for Lefty* and he was skinnier than I was. Next to Richie, next to those big biceps and the big nose and the big mouth, he looked a little nebbishy and sour. He was 4-F: a heart murmur.

"Sure, you can stay. I'm going out for another quart."

"Champagne of bottle beers." Richie grinned and hoisted his jelly jar. "Thanks, man." Jean-Paul didn't grin back.

* * *

Five years later we moved to Brooklyn ourselves. Back then, when you could still afford it, Park Slope was the destination for all the refugees, all the failed artists and actors and opera singers, and it was crawling with radicals too. Even when I had babies I had a lot of downtime to wander, to search for Richie in the health food store and the big library at Grand Army Plaza and on the ball fields in Prospect Park. I looked all the time, at any tall swarthy male, and for a while I started to see him behind beards and under yarmulkes and once, even, beneath a Sikh turban. I bought every Springsteen album, to study the pictures, because Bruce had the same moves as Richie and I had an idea they'd age the same way. Every time I heard a siren in the night, I saw F.B.I. agents cornering him, pulling him away from his new life as a social worker or a labor organizer. Sometimes the last thing I saw before I fell asleep was Richie behind prison bars, springsteening to imaginary music.

He wasn't in Park Slope anymore, or I would have seen him. I would have known him even if he'd had plastic surgery or dressed as a circus clown. He was probably up on some farm in New Hampshire or out in the Northwest working a fishing trawler. When they started finding people in the '90s—Sara Jane what's her name—I held my breath. I knew what I was doing. Dreaming about Richie, fixating on him, was the safest fantasy a long-married mother of three could possibly have, and anyway I only used the idea of him when Jean-Paul and I were so sick of each other we could spit, or kill each other, or both. Then I'd start looking all over again: he was the one, my grand passion, my Heathcliff, my Vronsky, my-roll-me-over Romeo, my Cool Hand Luke. As long as he hadn't blown anybody up. I bought every book on the last days of the SDS to look for his name, but after September 11th I couldn't even turn the pages. Anyway, I never found his name.

But I found him, one rush-hour morning when I wasn't looking at all, way down at the front end of the subway platform, the Manhattan-bound Q, wearing a well-cut suit. Very well-cut: Armani, maybe. It could have been a million prosperous guys and it could only have been him. I moved down the platform for a better look, but the train pulled in and I only had time to focus on a manicured left hand, holding the door for a woman in a tight skirt. No wedding ring—but then Jean-Paul and I didn't wear wedding rings either, because the ones we bought in the Village were so cheap they split the first time we slammed our hands down in anger. My shortness of breath alarmed me.

I began to see flashes of him everywhere: in the Key Food if I ran in for a quart of milk, coming out of Ozzie's with a cup of coffee. He was always dashing away—avoiding me? Still hiding? I was sure it was Richie. That nose, and the same wavy hair, graying and receding now, but scissor-cut, feathered, long on the neck. An expensive haircut, and an expensive suit, more of a disguise than a Sikh turban. I mean, the Richie Daccapo I knew tied his hair back with a piece of dirty string.

* * *

The Richie Daccapo I knew lived next door on Long Island, in Hicksville (no kidding), and when we were five and six and seven you couldn't have pried us apart with the jaws of life. I don't even remember going to school when I was that age, I only remember running with Richie out to the hot empty fields where I stood with my wooden bat, pretending I might actually hit the ball, while Richie threw faster and faster and I swung late every time. We were six-year-old lovers, more in tune with each other than anybody who's ever passed through the dark night of puberty. Not that it was sexless: it was all sex, pulling down shorts behind rhododendron bushes to show each other body parts and touch them and maybe even kiss them: the taste of salt, the smell of my mother's Clorox. When she threw me into the tub at night she snapped, *Don't touch yourself, don't touch your body. What have you been learning from that boy?*

My mother called the Daccapos *coarse*: the *language*. Their *frig-gings* floated through the patio doors, and Richie's father wore a sleeveless undershirt—how coarse could you get? Actually it was one of the few fashion differences between him and my father who had, by coincidence, also gone to Fordham night school. Now they were numbers guys (Mr. Daccapo an accountant, Mr. Feeney an actuary), steady faithful family guys who rose at five-thirty to catch the six forty-five. They always had a pack of cigarettes within hand's reach (Winstons for Feeney, Marlboros for Daccapo), the Zippos lying on top. Richie alternated whose lighter he stole.

We were the gang leaders, Billy the Kid and Pocahontas, hiding in small places, clinging to each other. *Where's my frigging lighter?* Our fathers lay on their couches, dead men listening to Huntley-Brinkley and cough cough coughing, thick yellow phlegm, exhausted worn-out coughs. We crouched between the couch and the wall, squeezing each other, squeezing the Zippo. Maybe we already knew they weren't going to make it. Richie's father dropped dead of a heart attack on the Long Island Railroad when he was forty-four years old. Five years later, my father went in for the chest x-rays.

I can see Mr. Daccapo out in the back yard, the dark hair lush under his arms. He's standing by his new gas grill, his altar, one hand on the cover as if to assure himself that it's all his, or maybe to give it a secret blessing. I'm ashamed to look at him. He just stands there in the dead center of the yard, touching his grill, blissed out. Finally he lifts his hand to shake a Marlboro from the pack and tear the filter off. He's a goner.

* * *

I had to shake Jean-Paul awake—all that beer—and when I said Richie was down on Broadway just about naked, gonna get himself killed, he looked at me with that blank look he had already perfected. I said: "OK, OK, I'll go myself, only don't yell at me if somebody drops a bottle on my head." The Upper West Side still had SROs on every block, and the winos dropped their empties out the windows. My mother couldn't believe we lived like that.

"I'll go," he said, in that male-dog voice, that low flat growl that says *I'll go* and means *and if I catch up with him I'll kill him while I'm at it.*

I watched from the front window but soon enough Jean-Paul slipped from sight, jogging east. I was surprised to see him running: I thought he'd just walk around the block once and come back to say Richie was long gone. At this hour even Broadway was deserted, open season for the muggers.

After forever the two of them came back into the frame, Richie stooping, trying to hide his tall nakedness behind short Jean-Paul. My guilty little heart beat hard. We'd only been married five months and already I was comparing one body to the other.

Richie was wild-eyed when he came through the door in his underwear, exhilarated, drunker than when he'd gone to bed drunk. "This guy frigging saved my skin." He put an arm around Jean-Paul's neck, but Jean-Paul picked it off: a bug, a louse. "Your old man hauled off and hit me."

"Somebody had to stop you. Where'd you think you were going?"

Richie collapsed on the couch, groaned and laughed till something came out of his nose. "I have no frigging idea. Listen man, thanks for coming after me. Cause if they picked you up with me. . ."

We were all wide awake, taking that in. Richie pulled on jeans over his holey BVDs. With his hair down and just the one lamp on, he looked younger than he had all night, maybe a little panicked. "And Feeney, thank God you knew what the deal was—she ever tell you about her sleepwalking days? She was famous for it, man. She used to make *tracks*."

It was true. I did make tracks: I ran for my life. I'd wake in a sandlot circling the bases, my parents' robes flapping behind me. They screwed bigger and bigger chains higher and higher on the front door, but no chain could hold me: I dragged a stool over and I busted out of stir. Someone always heard the scrape across the floor, someone always tore downstairs after me, but always too late, always a swing behind. I was gone, I was out of there.

I was eight, nine, ten those sleepwalking years, the years when the gang split in two, when some of the boys could actually hit Richie's pitches and I was stuck with the girls and their pointy-breasted Barbies. My mother didn't understand why I punished my dolls with needles and buried them up to their necks. Next door Richie and his men put all their green toy soldiers in the new grill with firecrackers and watched them pop-pop-pop, privates goo-ing all over the rack: excellent practice for the militant wing of the SDS. That night we heard Mr. Daccapo *frigfrigfrig*ing at the top of his lungs, and once we saw him chase Richie down the street with a broom, Richie's voice rising and falling and cracking, a little sob at the end when his father caught up with him.

"I get it," Richie said. "For sure. I'm in Feeney's pad, I associate Feeney with sleepwalking, I sleepwalk myself."

"I'll put the chain on." I knew a chain wouldn't hold Richie either, but when it was safe in its slot he closed his eyes.

Jean-Paul and I crept back to the little bedroom. "You really hit him?" Under the sheets, we lay a million miles apart.

"You're lucky I didn't strangle him."

* * *

The second time he left I heard him rattle the chain, just the way my parents used to hear me, but I was too late. The elevator was already whirring and Jean-Paul's shoes were already tied. He headed for the stairwell without a good-bye, as if he held me responsible for this sleepwalk of Richie's. Maybe I was.

This time I wasn't staying behind. I slipped into sneakers that had long since lost their laces and took off after them. I was wearing what I wore day and night in 1971: an Indian bedspread I'd scooped out and tied around my neck, no bra in the daytime and no panties at night. In the dark of night, I could get arrested too.

I had no idea which way they'd gone so I followed a hunch and headed south on Broadway. At 105th I thought maybe I saw them on the east side of the street, two guys trucking along one after the other. I broke into a noisy run, my loose shoes slapping the sticky sidewalk. It was a cool, twitchy, muggy night. Broadway smelled of rotting vegetables. The harder I ran, the harder it was to breathe, but up ahead Jean-Paul had almost caught up to Richie and I had almost caught up to the pair of them.

I put on one last push, but as soon as I was within reach I spied a cop hanging out at the top of the subway stairs across 96th Street. I slowed to a walk just as Richie, barefoot and bare-chested, his pants sliding down his hips and his hair frizzing out, walked right up to the cop and clasped him on the shoulder. Was he awake? Was he turning himself in?

I thought that Jean-Paul would turn around then, but he was a steady faithful guy and he never missed a stride. Crossing 96th, he followed Richie right up to the cop and put his own arm around Richie's shoulder. From my shadow I could make out a pale wary hand flexing on a nightstick.

They stood there forever. I planned my run back home, my calls to find a lawyer for the fugitive and his accomplice. My mother would die. I hadn't said a real prayer since eighth grade but I heard myself chant *Hail Mary* three times, fast. Lo and behold, the cop swept Richie and Jean-Paul down the street with both hands and then sauntered away.

I reversed course, shamed that I hadn't gone to back up Jean-Paul, and scooted from shadow to shadow till they caught up with me. Then we walked home together after all, wordless till we crossed 105th and Richie keened: "What am I frigging doing? What is this, like a death march?"

"*Death march* is a little melodramatic. Let's just shut up till we're back inside."

We didn't even talk on the elevator. Inside, the door safely latched, Jean-Paul enunciated every word as if Richie were hard of hearing or stupid or both: "What we're going to do is we're going to pile stuff in front of the door." He got to work on a fortress of books and LPs while Richie and I sat stunned on the couch. Pretty soon he had most of our worldly possessions blocking Richie's path. He topped off the pile with the banged-up pots and pans from his father's restaurant, to clang out if Richie got anywhere close.

Richie still didn't look fully conscious. "Time is it, four-thirty? I better sit up, man. How could I do that, go looking for a pig?"

"You don't have to sit up. You're not getting out of here." Jean-Paul played the line just right, world-weary, and exited for the bedroom.

Richie let a long shudder run the length of his body and picked up my hand to lay it on his chest, so I could feel his heart galloping. Then he leaned his head back into the cushions and pulled me close. He tripped his fingers through my hair, curling it strand by strand the way he used to when we sat on the back steps. Our breathing slowed, our breathing sped up.

"What'd you say to him?"

"The cop? I said *Peace, baby*. Your *husband* told him I was a frigging frat boy at Columbia who'd had too much to drink."

"Just don't go blowing anybody up, Richie." I snuggled into him the way I used to all those afternoons after his father died and we sat out back trying to make sense of the world.

"Feeney, Feeney." I felt myself melt into him. "What if I have a frigging breakdown? What if you have to take me to the emergency room?" I could feel more than his heart rising. He took my hand to lay it on his jeans, on his doggy cockiness. He wasn't so scared after all.

From the bedroom the springs squealed: Jean-Paul shifting on the mattress. Only the little kitchen separated us. He could hear every word Richie groaned out, and every word I answered. I jumped up and made my way back to our bed without another word. It was as if I were sleepwalking too, only this time I came back home, locked myself in safe and sound, and nobody even knew I'd gone missing.

Jean-Paul finally deigned to say one word, enunciated precisely, delivered without an excess of feeling: "Asshole."

* * *

How could I tell Jean-Paul that Richie was the smell, the taste of my child-hood? It wasn't something you told your husband, it was something you swal-lowed, and once it was down your gullet you could keep other secrets too. How could I tell Jean-Paul that all I dreamed of, for weeks before we married and months after, was Richie Daccapo?

One dinnertime the Daccapos got a knock on the door from an L.I.R.R. man. From the Feeney house we heard Richie's sisters scream out *No no it's not true it's not true.* Even my mother, accustomed to high opera next door, was alarmed. She peered through all the windows trying to see what was going on. I stood behind her and watched Richie tear out the back door and make his way across the yard to the grill, the altar, the holy site. I thought he was going to put one hand on the cover, the way his father did, but instead he hammered it with his left fist. His pitching arm. I didn't once think about what I was about to do. I tore out of my own house, down the stairs, out the back door, through the rhododendrons. I hugged Richie from behind, hugged him with all the breath in my body. I knew it was his father, I knew his father was a goner, I'd known it all along. How could he not have a heart attack, running after Richie with a broom? For a while Richie kept punching the grill even with me hanging on his back, but I could feel him slowing down because I was there, because I wrapped my arms tighter and tighter around his waist. After a while he stopped and shook me off.

"Why'd he make all those jokes about colored people, why'd he have to do that?"

"I know. My mother hates Italians even."

He went back in the house without another word and I went back next door and after another while you could hear them all settling down. "I'm sorry he walked away from you like that, Joan." My mother had watched everything.

"Good grief," my father said. "His old man's dead. He's supposed to stop and chat?"

"I know you haven't been the best of friends with Richie lately." My mother ignored my father as usual. "I know the family's coarse."

But when we walked into the wake Richie rose to comfort me, as if I were the mourner, and hugged me frontways, the proper way, the way we used to hug when we were small. And that was that, we were back, flesh against salty flesh, forever and always, fourteen and fifteen and sixteen, grieving Richie Daccapo the man of the house, his mother and his sisters driving him out of his frigging mind but me Joan Feeney right next door, ready to snuggle and cuddle and smooch. Whatever we did, we wouldn't turn into our parents.

The night of our graduation, Richie told me I was crazy to go to the college both our fathers struggled through, night after exhausted night, a Jesuit school. *You ought to get out, man, get real, get away from the frigging priests. Come to Madison, we'll bust the place open.*

* * *

I'd been seeing him for months without his seeing me so maybe it shouldn't have surprised me that Richie had to get right up in my face while I was eyeballing paperbacks in the window of Community Books. "Feeney, I don't believe it. What are you doing in Brooklyn?"

"I live here." It was so anticlimactic: a Yankees cap on a Saturday afternoon. He looked ten years younger than I did—tanned, oiled, massaged—and his hug was gym-toned.

"Hey, so do I. Got myself a sweet brownstone in a recession sale." His Long Island accent, I noticed, had been diluted. The neighborhood where all the failures and the lefties came, thirty years ago, was full of guys who could afford Armani now. Richie got handsome when he got old, even surer of himself if that was possible. I was a wreck—my straw hair was woven with gray, and I wasn't skinny anymore—but he leaned against the plate glass with all the time in the world. "It is so good to see you."

I sucked up every syllable. "What do I call you now?"

"You can call me Richie. You're the only one I'd let get away with it."

"No, I mean. . .you didn't change your name?" He looked at me as if I'd lost my wits. "When you went underground?"

He leaned his head back against the glass—you could hear a little *clunk*—and howled. "Oh my God."

"You didn't go underground?"

He wiped his eyes with the same fist that once slammed into his father's gas grill. "I played at hiding out for about three weeks, and then I hightailed it back to Madison in time for finals. I was living in this neighborhood, actually, those three weeks. '72? '73?"

"It was '71. Weren't they looking for you, wasn't there a warrant?"

He shook his head. "Two of my, uhm, buddies got nabbed in a stolen car. That was a nasty business, I regret that. My prints were all over everything. I was convinced they were looking for me. . ."

He saw the look on my face and lowered his voice: "My friends had plastique." I'm not sure exactly why I didn't believe him, but my heart swooped the same way it used to when I saw him sidling up to other girls. Plastique was supposed to evoke Euro-terror, Baader-Meinhof and the I.R.A. Richie wanted to paint a hyperromantic picture—as if I needed help with that.

"But you made it back for finals."

"And into law school without a black mark to my name. Hey, what about you? What you doing with yourself?"

No underground? No arrest warrant? *Law* school? One day he was fooling around with lightweight explosives and the next day he was studying torts? "I teach."

"Acting?"

I realized then that I hadn't finished the sentence because I didn't want the well-dressed attorney to know what I did. "Middle school. You know, I thought maybe I saw you one morning on the Q."

"Wish I'd known, would've bought you a cup of coffee. I can't tell you how many times I've told the sleepwalking story. Maybe I could buy you that coffee right now."

I said I was sorry, I couldn't, though I had time to kill, my children long gone and Jean-Paul off at the restaurant. Immediately I regretted turning him down—who was being the snob? "Why don't you come over for a meal? Come tonight. Bring your family."

He did a little Springsteen swivel. "No wife at the moment, and the girlfriend's travelling. Might be a good night for catching up."

* * *

When I called Jean-Paul on his cell, to tell him Richie Daccapo was coming to dinner, he said: "Who's Richie Daccapo?" But he remembered well enough when Richie showed up at the front door, or maybe he remembered how Richie affected me. The two of them started pawing the ground over drinks—too many drinks—and the three of us staggered through the apartment to the dinner table.

I was shocked at my middle-aged heart, thunkathunking over this guy I used to love. Jean-Paul doused him with questions and Richie gave a lawyer's cautious answers: he'd been divorced for ten years now, his girlfriend was in Singapore, closing a deal. Jean-Paul wouldn't let up. Big firm? Been there long? Richie rolled his eyes, calculated: "Let's see. . . I made partner in '83." I blanched. For twenty years I'd been seeing him on a fishing trawler.

"You're a litigator?"

"Mergers and acquisitions. I live and die by the numbers." Richie flashed an ironic smile in my direction, to remind me that I might have turned the corner on fifty but I was still a teenage girl.

Jean-Paul had thrown together the food, though he rarely cooked at home: he was a chef now, in his father's restaurant. We were working our way through avocado and endive, or at least Jean-Paul and I were. Richie had swallowed his salad down in two bites, as if to show how puny it was. He was giving Jean-Paul as good a third degree as he got: Where was the restaurant? How many reviews? How many stars? Jean-Paul spluttered at *stars*. Pascal was a little café on the edge of Hell's Kitchen that had somehow survived for forty-five years, most of Jean-Paul's life and all of our marriage. Actors went there. "I'm not usually home Saturday night. Joan insisted."

Richie gave me a wink to suggest I should have insisted the opposite. "Whatever happened to the acting biz?"

"We were bad actors. Anyway, I was. Jean-Paul did—"

"Commercials, voiceovers." He left it at that, left out how he went to Madison Avenue in the '80s and got laid off just after we bought the apartment, left out that going back to his father was the hardest thing he'd ever done. We had three children by then. He sized Richie up again, from his end of the table—he'd sat him down at the opposite end, so they could stare at each other properly. "You have kids?"

"My partner makes maternal noises from time to time, but I'm not sure I could bring any more kids into the world after 9/11."

That shut us all up. We didn't do the *where were you* thing—we'd done it once too often. I'd never once dreamed that Richie Daccapo might be downtown in a white-shoe law firm. Finally I said: "Our oldest, Paul—he's in law school, you might appreciate this—got busted down in Washington, protesting the war. His dean really made him sweat it."

"I guess he won't make that mistake again," Richie said.

Jean-Paul said: "What mistake?"

"Mistakes of our youth." Richie gave me another almost-wink, but Jean-Paul was not amused. He got hot at the dinner table, even without Richie Daccapo sitting down at the other end. His family had always chewed up religion and politics with their meals, the subjects forbidden in the Feeney household, and sometimes I thought that was why I married him. He cracked our windshield with his fist when he heard on the car radio that Reagan had fired the air traffic controllers. Our kids called him the Last Socialist. He was the guy who stayed up all night emailing urgent appeals for prisoners on death row. Now the Last Socialist calculated if he could take the Corporate Lawyer. "You think it was a mistake, protesting Vietnam?"

Richie raised his glass. "Here's to the sixties. Here's to those protests."

"You don't want to toast the protests these days?" Jean-Paul had just about worn himself out over Iraq. He'd been to every march, got penned in on Second Avenue, had a mounted cop rear up on him—just like the old days.

Richie flashed a rueful smile. "These are different days. A kid in law school's got to be careful."

"I can't believe it. After the kind of trouble you—"

Richie scraped his chair around, ducked his head in a way that was supposed to be modest and charming. "I was full of myself."

"Well, our son's not full of himself."

"That's not what I meant."

"What did you mean, exactly?" You could almost hear the two of them growling. They'd stopped turning my way with winks and nods. They were only bearing down on each other. I was invisible: the middle-aged woman, the middle school teacher, the monkey in the middle.

Richie pretended he was searching for the right words. "Anybody who plans to take the bar has to be cautious these days. After 9/11. . ."

"After 9/11, maybe he feels the urgency."

"Ah, youth. I remember. . ."

"What do you remember? Being *on the lam?*"

"Well what do you remember? *Letters to the editor?*"

"After 9/11," Jean Paul said, and now you could see that his heart was the one thunkathunking, "it's a pity to raise the body count."

"My, you are the unrepentant liberal, aren't you?"

It might have been the way he said *my*, the way he made Jean-Paul sound so quaint and old-fashioned and womanish. Or maybe it was the *liberal*. Jean-Paul took his time, inhaled a deep actorly breath. "I said back then that you jerks would be working for the Bank of America."

"I don't work for the Bank of America. I'm with Feckersham Wilton-berry Raft." It was supposed to be a joke, I think.

"It was all just a rush for you, wasn't it? Making like you were out to save the world when you only wanted a cheap thrill."

Richie snorted. "*Cheap Thrills* is a classic and Joplin's a saint. Otherwise, I don't know what you're talking about."

"You know exactly what I'm talking about. What's a few innocent by-standers when this building blows? What's a few hundred workers laid off in this merger? What's a few Iraqi kids under this bomb?" Jean-Paul had delivered his share of wine-induced diatribes over the years, but he'd never been quite so sweeping. He rose, to make the pronouncement official. "I'll have to ask you to leave. I don't want any neo-cons sitting at my table."

"Hey now, did you hear me say I was a neo-con? I'll have to ask you to stick to the facts as you know them."

"The fact is, you were willing to get us busted right along with you. And now you criticize our son, who's out there putting his ass on the line."

"I don't like your tone." When Richie rose from his own chair the room got still, but I could hear the little crackle you hear just before the light bulb explodes. I watched Jean-Paul hoist up his end of the table, watched the restaurant crockery and glasses go sliding down toward Richie. The hollandaise drooled onto his Saturday night black jeans: the only piece of clothing on him that Springsteen might have worn. Richie picked up the plate with the last clinging avocado slice and flung it back the length of the table, where Jean-Paul ducked precisely in the nick of time. His stage training. He crouched beside the table, waiting for more lobs. "You were sleepwalking through Vietnam, too."

Richie found another shard to hurl, hesitated. You could see him consider heaving the little guy, pitching him through the window. Then you could see him calculate the cost. He released a slider and turned his back. "Not the best reunion, Feeney," he said. "Next time, my place."

Jean-Paul hurled a wine glass from his hiding place, but it didn't get close. "Not going to be a next time, asshole." Richie was already halfway to the door, and then we heard the latch click.

"I'm glad you got that out of your system."

My husband rose painfully on his bad knees and beat his Wild Man chest. "I should have kicked him out thirty years ago, before he kept me up the whole damn night."

"I'm sorry, Jean-Paul." Meaning, I think, sorry about that night, about this night, about all the disappointment and bitterness we had accumulated through the years. Maybe I was sorry I was a middle-aged woman who still saw herself squeezed between two twenty-year-old boys.

"Well, I'm not sorry." He scooped everything into the tablecloth, the way they would have done at Pascal. He was exhilarated. "I've got a long list of people I'd like to throw a few dishes at. All those loudmouths who used to be leftier than thou. Why don't you invite Paul Berman to dinner? David Horowitz?"

* * *

An hour later he was still pumped, full of adrenaline, ready to take off. From bed, twisting in the sheets, I watched him at his email. We ran a two-shift marriage, one of us always asleep before the other, but a long marriage too: a steady faithful family guy. A miracle he lived to be older than my father got to be.

We had a bad stretch in the eighties. I sleepwalked through that time, literally: I wanted out of there, out of town. I went from bed to bed, touching my children's foreheads. The next morning they told me how they woke to see their mad mother staring down, tracing their faces. One or the other always walked me back to my own bed, back to my husband's side. Gracie, our middle child, caught me one night leaving the apartment. I was in my nightgown but I'd thought to grab my wallet.

"Why you think he went right up to that cop?"

Jean-Paul didn't even stop typing. "Wanted to get caught." Not a second's hesitation. "Wanted somebody to stop him."

The way I went to my children's beds, so they would stop me.

But nobody stopped Richie. After his father died, his mother bought him a little Fiat convertible with the insurance money, and he raced it faster and faster down the Long Island Expressway. *Please Richie, not so fast.* I never said it out loud: maybe I didn't want to go that fast, and maybe I did. *Please, you're gonna get us killed.* Ninety-seven, a hundred and two. *Somebody's gonna get hurt like this.* A hundred and five, one-ten. He was the coolest guy in high school, the alpha male, girls hanging off him: he even got elected vice-president of the Afro-American Society, though he didn't actually go to the meetings. I picked the one who went to the meetings, the one who married me when my father was dying, the one who wrote the emails late into the night.

* * *

The third time he went sleepwalking that night, Richie knew better than to get near the pile of pots and pans. He crawled into our bed instead, the way he might have crawled in with his parents when he was small . . . or maybe he thought he was cavorting in some commune after all. When I woke at dawn he was pressed against one side of me, Jean-Paul against the other, their bodies rising with the sun: one heart racing, one heart murmuring, the heart in the middle ready to burst.

We were clinging to each other. We were kids on the run.

COMPANY

WHEN LILY CALLS TO SAY I should come talk some sense into Diego before he ends up destroying himself, I remind her that I've made a point of avoiding that sweet cheater for years and years now. He seems to have managed just fine.

"Fine? He's been on hunger strike since this last surgery."

What surgery?

She rolls it out as if it's old news: last week, after all those years of diabetes, they amputated again. I don't know about any diabetes, much less years of it. I don't know about any amputation. Vertigo swoops me up. Lily says that the surgeon is waiting to see whether the right foot will have to go too, so I stop listening entirely. While the world somersaults, I catch sight of a skinny leg hacked off mid-thigh: I see ribbons of bloody flesh and hear Diego—flâneur, lover of women, cock-a-doodler—howl.

* * *

Once upon a middle-aged time, reader, Diego O'Dowd and I lived together in an artists' co-op I'd founded back in the days when artists in downtown Manhattan bought decrepit lofts, unsafe at any price, with money they begged from respectable relatives. By the time Diego moved in, I was forty and Diego fifty, our marginal existences long established: my proper Southern mother had almost resigned herself to my unmarried, childless state, though I'm pretty sure she never resigned herself to Diego. We painted at opposite ends of the same studio where we slept, breathing in the toxic fumes of our art, and consoled each other about our rescinded charge cards, our adjunct teaching gigs, our dwindling shows. We ranted together about the torture regime Diego once fled. I even made a little film about his uninsured adventures in emergency rooms. We danced tangos, Diego counting time to keep me in step: ONEtwoThreefour.

At two or three or four in the morning, he returned triumphant from a night of bar-hopping and stood at the refrigerator door considering the sparse pickings. In the light of our antique icebox, his belly hung loose and easy, his skin darkening with the wine he'd downed and the moles that sprouted like mushrooms as he aged before my eyes. His appetite was insatiable.

And so was mine. Why, reader, did his flaccid arms and skinny legs make me so tender? Why did I crave his touch? Other artists had moved on—to video, to text, to performance—but Diego, who wasn't faithful to much, was faithful to paint. His colors were sublime. His subjects were women: nudes who morphed into fruits and vegetables, surreal mangos and artichokes in neon colors of such pure intensity that I prickled in their presence.

He bragged, he bellowed. He fretted about his grown daughter in Buenos Aires, but did he go to see her? No, he put a scratchy LP on the turntable, came to stand over our bed in the small hours of the morning, and held his hand out:

"Just one, Maisie, and then we sleep like angels."

I'd been sleeping like an angel till he woke me. I rose to dance.

When my little film about a swaggering artist sans medical insurance made it into Sundance, Diego fevered up with jealousy: *Your exotic Latin lover with empty pockets*, he sneered. *But maybe you'll make a dime off me.* When my little film won Best Documentary, he burned hotter still.

But all that was long, long ago, reader: another lifetime. Now I'm a retired Best-Documentary professor living in paradise. I have bought myself a marshside house in a Southern hometown I once fled the way Diego once fled Argentina. I've made my peace with Due East: Spanish moss festoons the live oaks outside my windows, porpoises swoop in my tidal creek. The light is as surreal and sublime as Diego's colors ever were, and for the first time in my life, I have all the time I need for paint, that old honest pal. I'm perfectly content, past the need for company I didn't invite, certainly past the need for tangos with pot-bellied cheating men. I held onto my loft, so I get to the city when I need to, but lately this place, this light, this stretch of time are all I need.

Only now Lily—Lily, of all people—has summoned me. I'm in a sufficient state of shock to run the numbers. If I'm drawing Social Security, that makes Diego seventy-six. Seventy-six? Unfathomable. In his seventies, on one leg, Diego's probably even behaving.

I indulge in an ugly sense of obligation, an overcooked, stewing-in-its-own-juices, Rivera-and-Kahlo, Picasso-and-his-many-mistresses, resentful-woman bitterfest before I get round to sitting at the computer and googling Rock Bottom Air. It has always struck me as a perverse name for a travel site, and the prices don't look all that rock-bottom to me.

* * *

I slip in while Diego's drooling and snorting. When he realizes someone's entered his dreams, he blinks and blinks again, cartoonlike. His hair's still thick for an old man's hair: it's gone past gray to a zincy white, and in his new emaciated state, flesh loops down his jaws. At the sight of me, he lets loose a brief delighted smile before he remembers where he is, what's happened, what might happen still. The other shoe, so to speak. The surgeon, Lily tells me, took his toes, then his foot, then his calf: this, it turns out, was the third surgery, the third mortification. Now, when he has nobody, I'm the lone volunteer, or maybe the lone draftee, to stand by this hospital bed. I contemplate the unlikeliness of Diego's securing a bed in the first place: if he's even bothered to signed up for Medicare, I'll know I've witnessed a miracle. He clamps his eyes shut.

"I ask for no visitors." Diego's English is perfect—he reads political theory in five languages—but he lives in the present tense. It's a Zen thing. He rings a buzzer he probably rings thirty times a day.

No nurse appears. I retreat to the visitor's chair and Diego, struggling his hips into a bearable position, retreats to dark silence. He's asked for no visitors to cover the absence of visitors. I think I can see, under the thin sheet, where they took the leg: just below the knee. I see his missing calf, too, its sparse hairs white as the hairs on his head, springing absurdly from a shin like a palmetto's trunk. I see his thick yellowing toenails, too much effort to hack through all these years. Now a surgeon's gone and hacked the whole thing. I want that leg. I want to paint it. What's the matter with me? Haven't I exploited him enough? That leg's no symbol, God knows, no metaphor. Its absence is as loud as the sad buzz of the fluorescent lights.

The nurse finally arrives, lumped into pastel scrubs, every inch of her lethargized by Diego's summons. "What's up, Diego?"

He won't even open his eyes: "Tell this lady to leave or I'll call my lawyer."

This lady. As if I'm some do-gooder who comes to harass him, to remind him that he needs to lose some weight, cut back on the drinking, stop picking up every downtown babe too nearsighted to see how old he is. He can't call a lawyer unless I pay the bill. What can I do? The nurse shrugs back: what can she do?

* * *

It's the same question I asked Lily when I walked in on Diego with a graduate student supposedly writing her dissertation on contemporary Argentine artists, though Diego hadn't had a solo show in years and the graduate student appeared to be an underage porn star. She was lying beneath him, naked on our rug—my rug—pierced everywhere with safety pins. He'd never been so flagrant before. He'd never been cruel.

After I kicked him out, I couldn't bear the city. I took my "Best Documentary" prize to a visiting distinguished-artist gig back home in South Carolina and proceeded through the stages of grief. I'd thought once that Diego and I would grow old together, that he would rub my arthritic shoulders. I knew how to live on my own—I'd lived on my own for a long time before him—but we laughed at the same jokes and railed at the same injustices. Reader, I liked his company.

Years passed, though, as years do, and after I parlayed my visiting gig into a permanent appointment in paradise, I managed to forget about Diego O'Dowd for days on end. Sometimes, drifting off to sleep, I pictured him humming Eladia Blásquez, rolling his hips lasciviously. I pictured him getting to work, whooping and going at it in a frenzy, in love with the brush in his hand.

And you, Lily used to lecture me, *are in love with the ultimate macho-man.* Lily (you may have heard of her, reader, the performing artist Lily Pons) is my oldest friend in New York, the one who founded the co-op with me. Lily gave up on men entirely at the age of seventeen, and the entire time I lived with Diego she despised him. But after I left she softened: she let him in to my place to pick up a brush he'd left behind, shared a drink with him when he brought back the key. Evidently he left a lot of somethings behind: over the years, Lily reported multiple sightings, reported that he'd sold a few big canvases, that now she railed with him about torture as practiced by his new country. Maybe she's even been letting Diego crash in my loft when I'm not there. The idea's strangely consoling, and gives me something real to offer Diego: he can stay in my place as long as he needs, rent-free, no subterfuge necessary, so that Lily can look in on him. When I leave the hospital, I knock on her door to let her know the plan.

She laughs sarcastically. Diego, she says, gets on her nerves. She is certainly not going to look in on him. "But you will," she says. "If I know you, you'll wait on him hand and foot."

Not the best expression, under the circumstances.

* * *

When I go back the next day, Diego's rage pitches higher. He hisses: "Go back to North Carolina."

I haven't corrected any New Yorker who inquired about *North Carolina* in years, but I correct this one. "You know perfectly well which Carolina."

"Go back there."

"I want to see the leg."

His lips twist. "Coño."

"I want to paint it."

I see the struggle of every vein in his neck. If there's one thing a painter understands, it's why another painter wants to paint some forbidden body part. He kicks the sheet off with his limbo leg. "Take your look, bitch."

In all our years together, Diego never called me such a thing, not in English. I get close, leaning low over the hospital bed to look at the stump, but there's nothing to see, nothing but strips of futuristic bandage leaking goo. I see anyway. I see where they sawed the bone an inch below the knee, where they left flaps of skin to cover gristle. The skin around his stump is wrapped neatly as a Christmas present, but the scar underneath will raise itself in one long angry welt, a fat line like a whiplash. Once they take those bandages off, the staples will shine. The flesh colors will be the muddy colors students use when they're starting out, though I see a pure light-infused green in there, a glint of old copper in Diego's scar. I move my hand to touch it—I'm not even aware of making the gesture, but Diego is. "Don't."

I don't.

This time, he doesn't bother to ring the buzzer or tell me, again, to get out. His eyes fill with such splattering pools of contempt that I pull the sheet up before he can stop me and leave him to his mourning. Have I mentioned, reader, that Diego cries easily, profusely? Have I mentioned that he once accused me of exploiting him?

The nurse tells me where to find the social worker, who explains that they're nowhere close to fitting him with any artificial limb, much less the titanium leg-of-the-future I've been fantasizing. Yes, Medicare will pay for a rehab facility for thirty days, and yes, he'll practice more on the crutches he didn't master the last time. Inconceivable, that you could overcome someone's despair in thirty days. The social worker—lumpy as the nurse but closer in age to me, closer in skin tone to Diego—looks as if she agrees about despair. Some woman like this must have done the Medicare paperwork for him.

"When he goes home," she says, "you'll have to—" I interrupt to offer my confession: I'm not Diego's wife. I don't live in New York anymore.

"Does he have somebody to look out for him?" We squirm together. She averts her gaze daintily to inquire whether I might be able to stay, just a few weeks, just to visit him in rehab and settle him back home, just till he can maybe get himself to the store for a quart of milk.

If I know Diego, a quart of Scotch is more like it.

* * *

Reader, the good former-lover swallows gall and stays. The good girl reclaims a loft allowing her this proximity to Diego who has no one. The good ex marvels at her prosperity, summoning the spaces she needs, rolling in retirement dough.

The night I spring Diego from rehab and bring him home to my place, I make chicken soup. For years, I watched Diego, insouciant in his chicken-butchering, make cazuela: I recall a hacked chicken, a bunch of carrots, onions, corn, potatoes. I tart it up with cilantro and chile. Too late I realize that I've made a Mexican, not an Argentine, cazuela and suspect that Diego won't appreciate a broad Latin bow.

Diego appreciates nothing, including the passive-aggressive home aide I realize I'm performing. So I slip out to buy a bottle of strictly-forbidden, wildly-overpriced Malbec and bribe him: if he sips my misbegotten cazuela, he can have a half-glass of wine. I realize perfectly well that I'm treating him as a five-year-old, that I'm using the lowest and possibly least effective blows in the Handbook of Mortal Gender Wars, but I won't watch him waste away. I water the wine and fool him: another miracle. Diego hasn't tasted wine in so long, it's moon-juice to him.

After he finishes two ounces of wine disguised as four, he opens his mouth as if to speak, but instead sips half a bowl of soup with a full measure of resentment. When he sets down his spoon he allows me to test his blood, surely calculating that this might buy him another half-glass of wine. It buys him the insulin shot he's been letting me inject for mysterious reasons. What could those reasons be, other than wanting after all to live? He howls:

"That soup is glue. You're the worst cook I know."

* * *

We drive each other crazy. We didn't, in the old days; or maybe when I drove him crazy then, Diego went and found himself a graduate student. I can't take him anymore, his unwashed smear of hair, his brown teeth. I can't take the city either: not the wind off the Hudson, not my moneyed neighbors, not the new glass-and-steel glitz of dear old dirty TriBeCa.

When the co-op's ancient boiler goes down and we've been two days without heat, I persuade him to board a plane, to stay awhile in the warmth of Due East. Reckless, I promise sun, and he snorts. In the old days, South Carolina was a concept that made him shiver: nobody with brown skin, he said, was safe down there. But that word *sun* gets to him. What he says now is: "Good a place as any to die."

Which is, after all, not so different from what every geezer in New York says, packing for winter in Florida. From what I said, heading south after Diego broke my heart. From what prompted me, newly respectable and newly retired, to buy a house on a tidal creek.

* * *

Some previous owner of my Due East house—*probably an artist,* the agent said accusingly—knocked out walls to make a big central room with an old-fashioned kitchen at one end. The space resembles a New York loft—my New York loft, as it happens—but this light's other-worldly. An endless bank of windows looks out on a shallow yard where, at water's edge, two live oaks poke through either end of a deck, gnarly limbs extended. The light slithers through a latticework of leaves and moss; sawgrass springs from the marsh beyond; the creek stretches out serene. To enter this house is to enter a peaceable kingdom, but Diego and I, exhausted, enter biting our tongues. Finally Diego says: "You pay big bucks for the water."

On either side of the house are a sprawling bedroom and bath, each wing with a lockable door. When I first saw the place, I pictured a recalcitrant teenager in one wing, or maybe an exiled errant spouse. The people who lived here could live together without living together, retreat always possible. How prescient of me to buy a house with two wings: retreat may keep me from murdering Diego. Within an hour, he's lying on the couch and complaining about the way my watercolor easel blocks his view.

"Go lie in the hammock."

"I can't get in the hammock much less out."

"How do you know if you won't try."

"You sound like my first wife."

First wife? I only know about one. Reader, I don't even ask.

* * *

Perhaps this return home is where you're rooting for a *getting-better-every-day* story, a *love-conquers-all* story, an *older-wiser-lovers* story. You can forget all that. Diego's catatonic twenty-three hours a day, and for the remaining hour alternates between rage and sarcasm. No, he won't see a shrink, a *Southern* shrink. No he doesn't care if he dies, he wants to die.

"What's the matter with you, Maisie, you don't see that?"

I drop sketchpads on low tables, buy a new tube of titanium yellow. Diego makes no moves in their direction. He makes as few moves as possible. Too much effort to fetch a knife or a razor blade; his plan is to disintegrate into dust and float away. Most nights, he doesn't make it back to the angry-teenager wing, but falls asleep on the couch, the T.V. blaring chase scenes into my dreams. He shrinks before my very eyes. I remember my time alone with sad nostalgia: a time when there was no one to resent, no one to punish.

You're not the one who's lost your entire identity, my mother lectures from the grave. *Tell him to shape up,* Lily barks from New York. *Duh,* the doctor says, and refers me to a social worker. I'm getting like Diego: I fold the name of the social worker and put it in my pocket, and a week later the name shreds in the wash like the dignity Diego's been shredding since I met him.

* * *

Lily calls to say the boiler's fixed and it's warm enough now to come back if we want. Diego hasn't said a word about going back—maybe, like me, he has dreams about a one-legged man tumbling down the subway stairs. He lets me drive him to the beach, to sit under a palmetto and listen to the ocean, but points out that our tree is rotting from the inside out, swarming with monstrous bugs. A buzzard circles, as if echo his ominous tone. The doctor says if he can hang on for another six months and keep those numbers stable, they can start thinking about a prosthetic. I watch Diego cringe.

He tries the hammock, but he was right: he can't get in, much less out. From the kitchen counter I watch him crawl to the picnic table to hoist himself up. I wait the requisite hours to look for the folding chairs, to persuade him to sit on the deck with me, but I don't know whether it's his pride or mine I'm salvaging.

"The water rises," he growls, and because the tide's going out, I know he means our planet, not our marsh. We sit together, lost in our exile, at the edge of the dying world. Pileated woodpeckers have sprung up in every tree, their mad percussion the closest we will get to a twilight tango. The first streak of sunset, Nehi orange, struts across our horizon.

I'm not sure Diego sees the sun setting, or the cormorants or the egrets or the Carolina wrens who have built a city in the pines that separate my property from the absentee landlord's next door. I wonder what that landlord thinks when he comes to check on his place after a Dreamvacation.com renter drives off. I wonder what the dream vacationer thinks: that we are an old married couple, I reckon, that I have stuck by my wounded vagabond of a man. Little does he know: I wouldn't say that desire still hounds me night and day, but I wouldn't say either that I'm out of its claws.

Diego, I believe, has escaped desire on one leg, and I don't think he will ever look back.

* * *

In the morning, he's crumpled on the couch as usual but I notice that he troubled to take his trousers off before he drifted—that's a new development. I creep closer to see if he's awake, to take my first long look at the stump since the hospital. I was right: that surgeon wrapped it neatly as a Christmas present. It's no stranger than a foot—reader, have you ever looked at an old man's foot?

I have my chance. Maybe it isn't my right—maybe I should ask—but I can't stop myself. That stump is as beautiful to me as Diego's body ever was. I bend to kiss it, and Diego, deep in the sleep of despair or release or resignation, doesn't so much as stir. You tell me: does this last transgression signal that I'm still exploiting him?

Diego farts his answer, the way Diego would, and beyond him the marsh stirs to life: the algae blooms, the sawgrass struggles to breathe, the oysters squeeze themselves in disbelief. I know perfectly well what will happen if he stays. The time to paint I've so jealously amassed will be wrenched away as I fetch pills and prepare injections and hide wine. I'll witness every second of his decline. I'll watch despair, the unforgivable sin, take the form of flesh— and I'm not entirely certain whose flesh will succumb first.

Resentment sends my heart clattering, but in the marsh, the birds consult each other about the weather—an afternoon storm, maybe?—and decide to go about their business, which is not the dying planet but their prospects for breakfast. Reader, what can I do? I go about my business too. I spoon the coffee.

The room fills with light, with the yeasty smell of Diego, the sound of coffee dripping: ONEtwoThreefour. I perch on a stool at the edge of the world and let my eyes rest on the horizon. I don't have much time, and I have all the time in the world.

A FREAK OF NATURE

THE FIFTIES. I DON'T REMEMBER MUCH—I was a small child—but I do know that fear was always buzzing in the background, like static from a transistor radio: a jangly jazzy fear, not altogether unhappy.

The day I discover I'm a freak of nature, the thrill runs from my belly button to my throat. We've come to see Dr. Freitag about the mysteries in my mouth, and he's found two whole sets of teeth up there in my top gums waiting to claim the space when my baby teeth fall out. TWO ROWS OF TEETH. The current jolts me, sitting there in his big red leather chair, a princess on my throne. Not everybody gets a spare set of teeth.

But my mother squints and blinks at the x-ray film, and when she finally makes out all my extra teeth she moans, "Oh my God," the way she did when she heard that Sister Alma's boils were cancer of the face. That's when I understand that I'm a monster. That's when I see how I'll have to curl my lip, how the prissy girls on the playground will lift their pink chiffon skirts and shriek at me.

Dr. Freitag says we must go to Charleston. For special shoes and my father's assistant principal suit we go to Savannah. For special doctors, like when my mother almost lost the baby again, we go to Charleston.

"It couldn't be polio-related, could it, Herb?"

Dr. Freitag rubs his big belly and cackles. Out in the colored waiting room, his parrot Lucinda lets out a cackle too. "Doris, you take the cake, and I mean the twelve-layer cake. Sweetheart, you just nervous about this baby, all the trouble you've had. Fanny, don't pay her any mind."

"Don't you tell Fanny not to pay me any mind."

"Y'all excuse me, I've got to go turn the x-rays off."

When he's halfway out the door my mother rubs her own belly. "We needn't to worry about polio, Fanny. The way he forgets that machine we'll all be dead of radiation time we're forty anyways." She's raised her voice and I'm already dead, from the shame of having a mother who says what she thinks. *Don't say Jewish, don't say Jewish, don't say Jewish*, I pray, though I'm not exactly sure what *Jewish* means. My mother wouldn't even know it if she broke Dr. Freitag's heart.

* * *

I've fled Herb Freitag's office and now I run for my life through the alley and down to the docks, peeking over my shoulder every few feet to see how much ground my mother, in hot pursuit, is losing. Our feet pound out a desperate rhythm on the old rotting boards, the bay sloshing beneath us, and every time we come to a knothole we miss a beat. She could trip and lose the hat she holds to her head, or even the baby. I take pity on her and let her catch me, though my father says I run like the devil and if I wanted to I could be over the bridge and onto the islands by now. My mother leans over, precarious, and the fake ostrich feather quivers atop her head as she stretches to deliver that hard slap to my thigh (at home she uses the hairbrush, and not on my thigh). To spite her, I don't even flinch.

But then she's the one who takes pity. She tells me I won't go through life with two sets of teeth. They'll give me an operation, or operations, and it'll be scary—no, she's not going to deny that, because so many children catch pneumonia after the anesthesia. But we'll all say a rosary before I go under, and that should make it come out right. We'll be brave no matter what happens. "O Fanny, it's good training, sugar, because I mean to tell you it's scary going under the gas when you have babies, too. I'll be there behind you, little pixie. Little changeling-girl. We can't have you with two rows of teeth and those cowlicks too!"

Do you suppose you can possibly remember something as clean and as bright as I think I remember screeching to a halt on the docks that day? I couldn't stand it when she called me *changeling*. I used to chant *I hate you, I hate you, I hate you*, though it never occurred to my sisters to say such a thing. She pulled down our panties and used the back of the brush, only she was never going to do that to me again. I incited my brothers to riot. I was her match, and we both knew it.

* * *

"It couldn't be polio-related, could it?" I ask my father. I'm still such a freak I'm allowed to sit up front between my parents the whole way to Charleston. My mother likes it when I rest my hand on her big belly and I like that too, better than anything except maybe resting my head there to hear the swoops and the gurgles, which might be gas and might be the next one, a boy or a girl I cannot say. In the middle seat AgnesAnn and Teresa have Caroline between them. Willie and Martin are in the way- back, covered with filth already, and every five minutes one of them says, "I'm suffocating, I'm dying, help me, I can't bweathe."

"Girls! You cannot keep the windows rolled tight when it's ninety-two degrees outside. You cannot."

"My hair," AgnesAnn shrieks.

"You have to compromise," my father says, "and roll them down half-way." Will moans that he's going to throw up.

"Stop melodramatizing," my father calls to the back of the station wagon and we all count the syllables. My father speaks that way all the time, even on the baseball field when he's apt to bark out *Maintain your equilibrium, men.* To me he says: "No, Fan, it's nothing to do with polio. It's a genetic anomaly."

Anomaly sounds like a dread disease, a sickness of the blood. My frantic mother often calms me down, but my calm father makes me think I'm dying after all.

"It's no big deal, is what that means. Where do you want to go after we see the specialist? You're the patient. Pick three spots."

"Only one of them has to be Harvey's," my mother says. Harvey's is the restaurant where my parents can get a martini, which my father says is illegal like everything else in the godforsaken state of South Carolina. I could go to jail and never get rid of my freakish teeth, but my father reads my mind and says, "Don't worry, the mayor drinks there too. And the sheriff."

"OK, Harvey's. And the slave market. And the Battery." I pat my father's thigh under the steering wheel. He hands me his smoldering cigarette to rub out, which is almost as good as listening to my mother's belly.

When I raise my head from the ashtray the sun blazes off the yellowing marsh, the air prickles with road dust, the whole world waits to explode. Up ahead we'll pass between two rows of live oaks, the moss swishing down, a canopy of shade. *Hurry, hurry.* Soon we'll drive over the bridge with the little stone chambers where the fairies hide till nighttime and then we'll be in Charleston. *Hurry, hurry.* My father reads my mind again and speeds up till we're under black cloud-cover. The world darkens. AgnesAnn and Teresa roll down their windows a little way, and hot wind comes rushing in.

* * *

The surgeon doesn't have nearly so much time to talk as Dr. Freitag and there's no parrot in his waiting room, just Martin and Will raising holy hell. He makes a face at the sounds coming from his outer office and says I'll have surgeries, not surgery, a childhood of waiting for the monster teeth to ease down low enough to pluck, then a new battle plan after we see how the survivors drop in.

My mother says it will be like childbirth: I won't remember what it's like. If you did remember, you wouldn't show up the next time and then the poor babies would never get born. Already I think of my extra teeth as babies that are going to get dropped into the incinerator the way the last baby did, bloody roots sizzling in the flames next to little charred baby fists.

But that first day I get no gas and no flames, just my parents white-faced in the bright sun when, after the surgeon, they take us to the Battery so Martin and Will can clamber onto the cannons and fire on Fort Sumter. I'm supposed to be clambering too, only I hang behind with Teresa and AgnesAnn, shamed, and we overhear my mother moaning:

"We'll never get out from under now."

"Don't worry, Fanny," Teresa says. "You can't go through life with two sets of teeth! We'll find the money somehow." Teresa is the sacrificial one who always says she doesn't need any new clothes or shoes or second helpings. I look at her mournful encouraging face and take off, darting through park benches till my father, this time, catches me.

"Where do you think you're going?"

I won't look at him, I won't, I won't.

He has to bend to take my hand. I'm so short and so skinny that they're always saying I could blow away—and I did once, during a little tornado nobody saw but my mother, a *baby funnel cloud*, a whirligig that swirled me up in our backyard till my mother at the clothesline pulled me back down to earth. Now my father hangs onto me. The whole family has to go without clothes and shoes and second helpings just so I'll be normal but I'm never going to grow anyway so why don't I just join the sideshow? The next time the fair comes, and the greasy man with no teeth at all stands outside the sagging tent, beckoning. My father says you call them carnies, and don't get too close. Don't peek inside, it would break your heart.

I drop my father's hand and dash off to climb aboard a big cannon. The clouds over the bay gather in my honor, sulky and mean. A storm brews over Fort Sumter: the wind swoops, the palmettos rustle, the hairs on my arms rise up, defiant. I spread my legs wide so I can blast away.

* * *

At the slave market my mother takes wet diapers wrapped in waxed paper out from her giant pocketbook and scrubs Will's and Martin's faces and hands till they holler. Then she makes AgnesAnn do their knees. She can't bend anymore. My father lines us up, scrubbed, for the slave lecture.

"Remember, these were human beings, wrenched from family and forced to do whatever the plantation owners wanted them to."

"But Pat, don't forget, lots of times the owners tried their best to keep the families together—"

"They were ruled by the whip."

"In fact, the whip was very rare in South Carolina, very rare. Slaves were like family, and the climate was just like Africa."

My father glowers. "The idea that you could own another human being." He shakes his head, and we six shake our heads and hang them down, ashamed, ashamed, deliciously ashamed and relieved we were not born colored because if we were colored we would think about whips and shackles day and night.

Now we are allowed to walk through. It's an open-air market, with a roof above: I'm trying to get it right. Was the roof tin? I see straw but that, I think, is from some fairy tale. Brick pillars, or wood? Wood, surely. These days it's a tourist trap, with gewgaw stalls for the Yankee tourists, but then it was mostly empty, only an old lady or two selling tomatoes or cucumbers or a woven basket. A ghost hall, light stippling down.

We tiptoe, our tongues dry. We don't make eye contact with the fat colored lady: we don't want her to know that our eyes are already glistening. A crate's upended and we see a big young man forced to stand atop it, stripped naked for all to see, a whip curled in the auctioneer's hand. We are all six chilled up the spine. We are our father's children.

* * *

In Harvey's all the waiters are dignified old gents with crinkled white hair to match their white jackets. They only see my father once a year, but they always say, "Doctor! How you been down there in Due East?" I don't know why they think my father's a doctor. My mother says they call him Doc because he looks so distinguished in his assistant principal suit and because he can pronounce the French names on the menu. My mother looks pretty distinguished herself, with her pink straw boater pushed back over her curls. Lots of women don't wear hats anymore, but my mother says in her day you could tell a lady by her hat.

She tells us *don't look now* but there's the weatherman in the corner and we all count to three before we turn. He looks exactly like he does on the television my father brought home last summer. We still gather around it every night, and my father says the way we watch it is as much of a prayer as the rosary we say after. The weatherman's drinking a martini too. When they bring my parents' martinis in those very same royal glasses it occurs to me that maybe we aren't so poor after all, not for all my mother threatens to sell Tupperware and Teresa makes a big show of washing her panties in the sink so we don't have to buy her so many pairs.

After a few sips of martini my father says we should get anything we want on the menu, anything. Teresa runs her finger down the prices—she'll get a plate of hush puppies with not so much as a glass of tea to wash it down—and Martin and Will cry, "Meat! Meat!"

"Shush now." My mother laughs at them, balancing her hat as she leans her head back. "You'd think we starve you poor orphans." Only on the word *orphans* her voice drops down low, as if she's seen an apparition. Here she goes again. Lately she's been crying over anything we do and sobbing out that she just hopes she doesn't die in childbirth because we would feel such sorrow and ache then. Women don't die in childbirth anymore! It doesn't happen! My father says so.

"Stop now," my father says, "stop." But she juts her head out, like a turtle, to stare. Then she turns as white as she did out in the blazing sun. All four of us girls, sitting across from her, turn around to look.

It's a giant taking his seat. Really, it's a giant, and we all see him this time, not just my mother. He's twelve times my father's size, but he's wearing a suit just as normal as an assistant principal's suit, a blue seersucker suit same as all the Charleston men wear in the summer, only twelve times bigger. His hair's combed over to the side like my father's, too, but the giant's hair is sparse and oily like the carnie's. *Don't get too close.* His face looks smushed: his nose is a flattened streaked tomato, as if somebody stepped on him. Who would step on a giant? Maybe he has cancer of the face like Sister Alma. He sits down all alone to eat his supper at Harvey's and we all hold our breath to see if he breaks the chair. If he orders a martini, they'll have to bring it in a bucket. Caroline waves at him, only he doesn't see. My mother gasps.

"Just calm down," my father says, or at least I think that's what he says. He's whispering, and so is everybody else in Harvey's.

"Here's what we do." My mother is hissing. "I'll grab up Caroline, and Willie and Martin can hang onto my skirt. One of the girls can distract him—you, AgnesAnn."

"What?"

"Spill a glass of water or something. I'll get them out on the sidewalk, Pat, while you slip the waiter enough for the martinis."

My father groans, and AgnesAnn groans with him. My mother does this all the time now. The giant looks perfectly friendly—see, the waiter greets him like an old friend, and then turns toward our table. My mother whispers: *Tell him. Tell him.*

The waiter leans in above my father. "Some tall gentleman, heh?"

"Uhmhum," my father says, stiff and sad.

"Must be very nearly eight feet tall. You see him before?"

"Nununh."

"You hear about him, though."

"No, I can't say I have."

"Most famous man in Charleston. Come in here about once a month." The waiter doesn't even trouble to lower his voice. "Got a law practice specialize in colored people problems."

"Oh yes? "

"Fair man. Very fair man."

"You see, Doris."

That is too much for my mother, who jumps from her chair but forgets the part about grabbing up Caroline and Will and Martin. She pushes through the restaurant, which is not so easy with her belly that big, and the giant half-rises in his chair as if to give her a hand. She escapes him, though, and wends her way through table after table till she passes through the doorway to the illegal bar.

"Think she gone find the washroom all right?"

"She just needs a breath of fresh air. She's. . .expecting," my father says.

The waiter chuckles. "We know how the ladies get."

And then we all order our food, as if my mother has not fled the restaurant, as if she isn't part of this family anymore. My father leads us in
conversation about the miracle of television and what it must be like to be
the weatherman, and when we have exhausted that, we move on to Captain
Kangaroo, a saintly man, kind as my father. The food comes in waves, like the
tide, and we don't mention my missing mother, though every now and again I
remember how she lost the last baby. We all thought she was just carrying on,
till the blood pooled all over the front seat of the car and ran out the passenger
door. I wonder if she's sitting on the sidewalk in a pool of blood.

When Teresa's hush puppies land, I seize the moment to peek again at
the giant. He's stooped over his own plate—shrimp! a mountain of it, a giant-
size portion—and not just because his head is so high above the table. His
bones are bent, his back stooped, his neck hanging down from shame, the
way ours were hanging down in the slave market: only ours was the shame of
being white and his is the shame of being a freak of nature. I want to go sit in
his lap. I want to show my mother there's nothing to be afraid of. I wouldn't
actually tell him about the two rows of teeth, but if I opened my mouth wide
enough he would see, and I wouldn't mention that they were going to fix me.

The giant reads my mind the way my father does, and smiles, his own
teeth huge and crooked, a soft yellow like roses. He has four or five sets in
there. Nobody sees but me.

"That suit custom-made." Our waiter has brought dessert: vanilla ice
cream with sparklers, six cut-glass bowls he removes from the tray with great
caution, as if they're alive. We all sit in awe as the sparklers sputter and pop,
red and blue, the ice cream itself singing out a cheerful message.

* * *

When we come outside, blinking in the bright cloudy haze, my mother's
sound asleep in the hot car, all the windows rolled down but the door locks
depressed and the plastic seat covers hot and soft to the touch, as if they're
melting. Her hat's tumbled down and my father makes us all stand back while
he plucks it off the seat and rests it on her head. When he sets the paper bag
of food down next to her, she starts awake at the rustle, then stares as if she
doesn't have the least idea who he might be.

"Did the giant take the babies?"

We all laugh. She's joking!

"Everybody in." My father brings Martin and Willie round to the back and opens the tailgate. Then he comes back for me, to go in through the driver's side.

"Aren't you hungry?" I ask my mother. She squeezes my hand and when I look up I see the tears streaming down. I squeeze back, furious, and let my nails dig in.

My father lights a cigarette before he pulls out. He has to guide us through the narrow Charleston streets and then the gloomy Charleston highway, where the wrecks pile up: drunken marines and blown-out tires and people with bad luck who don't see they're running off the shoulder, into the muck. "Got to make tracks, chickpeas. Got to beat out this storm."

By then the sky's blistered with black cloudpuffs and the streets of Charleston are still. The birds have all found their shelter, and if we don't make it over the fairy bridge fast, we'll be trapped in this city. "I hate Charleston," I say.

My father says: "I think it's the specialist you hate."

"Don't tell her who she hates," my mother whispers.

My father drives on, over the bricked streets, past the walled gardens. Everybody in Charleston lives in a mansion, unless they're poor and live in a shack.

"If I die in childbirth," my mother says, "I suppose you'll marry her."

"Doris, stop melodramatizing. Women do not die in childbirth anymore."

"I would rather you did. I would rather the children had that mother than no mother at all."

"Doris, I will not have you scaring them."

"I want to go to the cathedral," she whispers. "I want to make my confession."

"Marry who?" Martin calls, all the way from the back.

"Nobody." My father speaks in a calm clear voice that roars through the station wagon. "We're not going to the cathedral and we're not going to scare the children." He drives on, his cigarette burning close to his finger.

"I'll put it out." I'm whispering. He doesn't hear me.

My mother sobs. "I want to go to the cathedral. Please. Take me."

"Let her go." Maybe I'm still whispering. He drives on. "Let her go to confession." My mother squeezes my hand. I never take her side.

"Fanny's the only one, the only one who sees what it's like for me."

I'm her match, I can run like the devil, and I'll never let her spank me again. My heart is murderous, monstrous. "She's scared." I can't stop myself, pleading for her.

My father drives on. We're almost up to the fairy bridge, almost, but here comes a yellow light. My father slows, but before the car rolls to a stop, my mother opens her door. She's out before the light turns red, before the tires stop turning. She runs on those little birdlegs, her hand to her hat and the rain spitting. Martin starts to cry, and then Caroline, and then Will.

AgnesAnn says: "There is no woman, sillies! Daddy wouldn't do that. There is no woman."

When the light turns green, my father slides the station wagon forward and we all sit stunned. He means to take us home, over the fairy bridge, down the narrow highway in the darkening night, through the woods and over the marshes, while our mother wanders the streets of Charleston with a giant abroad. And she hasn't even had her supper.

A great clamor arises, even from Teresa, even from AgnesAnn. We're all shrieking her name, our mama, our mama, a cacophony of miniature Doris-voices. In our terror, we've become our mother. I hear myself hiccup:

"She just wants to go to confession. She just wants to go. . ."

When my father turns the car around and goes back for her, she's waiting dignified at the curb, though the rain lashes down and the water slides in streams from her boater. Or am I making up that part, melodramatizing, hurling down lightning bolts to show how dazzling my mother was? Maybe she was only waiting in the wilting heat. Maybe she was trudging away from us, heading still for the cathedral.

She climbs into her seat and smiles down sweetly. Don't let her squeeze my hand again, don't, don't. From my lap she takes the brown bag of food my father's brought her from Harvey's, a doggie bag that any other time would make her cringe. But this dark night she opens it eagerly and removes a single shrimp, from which she takes a dainty bite. The thunder crashes around us as we cross over the fairy bridge into the night. Or maybe it doesn't. Maybe I don't need a storm to find sitting next to my mother thrilling. We never did go back to the cathedral for confession that night, but still all our troubles were forgotten, washed clean.

* * *

By the time she was done, my mother delivered nine babies who survived, and even I, the hippie flower-child, had four—but I'm not holding my breath for grandchildren. My daughter says she doesn't want to raise a child in Brooklyn, waiting for the F train to blow or bombs to burst in cafés, waiting for the waters to rise and the earth to strangle itself. I haven't told her that it's not just the terrifying world, it's your own selfish heart you question when you bring children into the world.

Over the years I asked again and again about that woman my mother invoked, but begrudgingly AgnesAnn and Teresa explained that there never was another woman, how could there have been, wasn't my father always around? Even when the baseball team had an away game he was home by midnight, and on Sunday mornings he stood at the back of the church, an usher resplendent in his assistant principal suit—then, hooray, his principal suit. I never entirely believed them. Sometimes I wished my father loved another woman. Sometimes I prayed for it. *You're a mean old shriveled witch,* I hissed at her. Later: *You're a racist, an anti-Semite.*

And then, when I gave birth myself, I thought I understood her whole: the loneliness of living with small children, of never being heard, the way I thought I'd been banished from the world, hushed up and locked away, a princess in a tower with no one coming to rescue me. I even thought I understood her paranoia—I was a little paranoid myself, when my children were babies.

Sometimes as I'm drifting off to sleep I feel my mouth crowded with another set of teeth and I can't open my jaw, can't get a word of warning out. Sometimes I wake with my head sliding across the pillow, listening for swoops and gurgles, sounds of life. All these years later I remember that one and only time I took her side, imagined her despair, and feel again that the years themselves are transmitting messages. The wars drag on, the air is electric, the world waits to explode.

THE OBJECT OF MY PREPOSITION

— In memory of Ken Saro-Wiwa —

He WAS A SHORT MAN, five-two or so, no taller than I am. Straight-away I mistrusted him.

"My family and I are coming from Rwanda." He would not meet my eye. He swept away imaginary dust from the seat I offered, waved off my offer of coffee, snorted when I said *then how about tea*. His feet dangled down from the big plastic clinic chair the same way mine did: like a child's.

I had not seen a Rwandan that short. Not that I had a large sample to compare—maybe twenty Rwandans had streamed into Greenglass after the genocide, with their children and their adopted children and any little ones they could grab up and pass off as their children, and they were all tall, even the Hutus in mixed marriages. Greenglass has been taking in refugees since the Vietnamese boat people: Lebanese, Somalis, Kurds, Cambodians, Croatians, Bosnians. The interfaith council gets them here, and then God help them. Last year a Kosovar kid slashed five black girls in the Greenglass Middle School lunchroom with a razor blade. We've had our share of suicides.

I took out a legal pad and wrote down all the business you record about people whose lives have been ripped from them—not that I believed for a minute that this man was Rwandan. I would have staked my job on it. But I played along, told him that so far we'd had good luck with judges moving things along quickly. His was a very late request but we'd see what we could do. I could have one of the attorneys interview him tomorrow, and meanwhile he might think about any kind of trauma that would help account for the delay. That was going farther than I was supposed to go.

He wouldn't look at me—he turned his torso almost to a right angle—but when I said he should bring all his papers when he came back, all of them, he swung around and stared hard, straight at me.

"We are not coming from Rwanda."

"Well, how long did you think it was going to be before somebody figured that out?" I didn't usually speak to the clients that way but then, the clients didn't usually treat me his way either.

He matched any evil eye my ex-husband ever cast my way and lifted his chin. "We are coming from Nigeria."

"Why didn't you say so in the first place?"

"Because I have heard that the lawyers speak only to Rwandans. Because I am not telling my private business to any busybody."

I drew my own chin up, offended that he expected me to confuse one suffering African for another. "Mr. Okapu, I am not a busybody. I am the case manager. I compile the information the attorneys will need to interview you." And I slashed through *Rwanda*, rather dramatically I admit, and wrote *Nigeria* in block letters big enough for him to read upside down. Then I affected a businesslike tone to indicate how uninterested I was in his private business.

"Perhaps you would be good enough to tell me the basis for your claim."

A minute passed, but I did not so much as tap my pen. Finally he said: "*Doctor* Okapu."

"Dr. Okapu, perhaps you would be good enough. . ."

"Write that I was helping Ken Saro-Wiwa."

The little man might as well have slapped me. I could not write a word.

"That is spelled—"

"Yes, actually, I know how it's spelled." I knew how it was spelled because for a long time, around the time of my divorce, I thought I had killed Ken Saro-Wiwa. I was part of an urgent-action network—*the do-gooders*, my husband Frank called us—that sent telegrams and letters for political prisoners around the world. The bulletins asking me to beg for Saro-Wiwa's life came thick and fast, and though usually I answered execution appeals like those the night they arrived, these I piled up by the computer with all the unanswered mail. Around that time I couldn't concentrate on anything but my plans to put ground glass in Frank's granola or to lob a hand grenade into his girlfriend's condo. I drifted off to take two-hour naps and showers while I plotted revenge. In the morning I woke dizzy with guilt—I had to write about that guy, that sorro-whatsis, but by then I was running late for work.

I never did write a letter, not one, never lifted a hand to phone in a telegram, because I was falling apart, because I was so humiliated those days after my husband betrayed me that I could barely dress myself, much less save someone. The *Efficiency Queen*, Frank used to call me. But I, who had recently been so competent, so on top of our three sons' flights back and forth from college and grad school and the dry cleaning and the lectures and the dinner parties—not to mention the urgent appeals—I the Efficiency Queen let the dirty linen pile high and the unanswered envelopes flutter to the floor.

And one morning not long after they sentenced him, I opened the paper and saw that they'd executed Ken Saro-Wiwa. How could that be, so soon? I let out a howl I can still hear ringing in my own ears. I'd done it. I'd let him die.

I can't say anybody I've told the story to the last couple of years remembers who Saro-Wiwa was: a big deal in Nigerian TV, a writer, the bulletins said, and he'd been organizing the Ogoni people to stop the oil companies from fouling up their tribal lands. The Nigerian government cooked up conspiracy charges against him and threw him in prison but everybody figured they wouldn't really execute a famous person like that, a guy who preached nonviolence. Then, while the whole world drifted off, they hanged him.

So now I was the one who couldn't meet the little man's eyes. "Are you Ogoni?" I was practically whispering.

He must have gone back to staring at the wall, because that was what he was doing when I finally had the nerve to look.

* * *

"What a fascinating guy!" Cornelia said as soon as the door clicked behind him. She'd recently arrived in Greenglass from New York, and I was still surprised to hear her breathing the enthusiasms of the Midwest. Already she'd ingratiated herself, learned to parrot the local accent. The powers that be had decided that even though there was no more money for poverty law there was money enough to hire Cornelia part-time to help me manage cases I could handle perfectly well on my own.

"What did you think was fascinating about him?" I strained for civility through the doorway. The space was so tiny—Cornelia and Dawn, the secretary, sat right outside my office—that we didn't even need to raise our voices. In fact, I had to concentrate on holding my voice down, to keep the contempt out. It wasn't even Cornelia's fault. I hated her because she was in her twenties, because she was blond and lush, because she wore lowcut clingy blouses so we could all see her perfect plummy breasts when she leaned over. I hated her most of all because she'd married an old slob who dumped his wife to take up with her. He'd been some official in the first Clinton administration, and now he'd accepted an endowed chair in our Poly Sci department, because out here in the middle of nowhere they would pay him kazillions of dollars and he could hide from the Scorned Woman, too. Cornelia was perfectly pleasant—she tried *really really* hard—and that made me hate her even more. She said *awesome*. In the Midwest, she picked up *super*.

"He was so secretive. Want to fill me in?" As if she hadn't already heard every word.

"I'll let Ted know," I said.

"Super. But if you want to give any work to Dawn or I, anything we can help you with. . ."

That was another thing that drove me crazy, that she'd gone to Wellesley and she still didn't know to say *if you want to give any work to Dawn or me*, though she'd been an English major and had a year of law school at Columbia behind her. She was going to finish her J.D. out here, once she and the sugar daddy were settled in. Meanwhile she pouted and sashayed when the interns, third-year law students, were in the office. Mostly she sat at her desk and shopped for on-line lingerie. I kept my mouth shut, because they had created this job for me, too, twenty-five years ago when I was married to the hot young professor they wanted to keep around.

Now my job was all that stood between the homeless shelter and me. *The homeless shelter and I*, Cornelia would have said. Dawn and I didn't even have B.A.s, but at least we knew what the object of a preposition was, and the lawyers had us proofread their letters and briefs to get the grammar right. When I was in my twenties I was raising babies and giving cocktail parties for geniuses, and I giggled with gratitude when the legal clinic hired me as a typist. I was the Saga of Another Generation—the mad housewife—but Cornelia is a New Woman, and soon she'll be a high-powered attorney in a push-up bra, just like the lawyers on TV. After a while, her voice floated through again. "Ted's going to have a lot of trouble with this one."

"Why do you say that?"

"Oh, Immigration's not going to touch Nigeria. They're not going to want to know about Ken Saro-Wiwa."

"You've heard of him?"

"That year I was in England"—she'd been at the London School of Economics—"the Brits were obsessed with Saro-Wiwa. And oil. They wanted it to be Shell's fault, not B.P.'s."

Mostly I hated her because she'd been everywhere, because she spoke like a twelve-year-old but had dined with Hillary Clinton, because she paid attention to everything. She was the most ambitious person, aside from my husband, I had ever met.

* * *

Ted Reilly, the immigration lawyer, was funny about Okapu. He was going to file for asylum, all right, but meanwhile he had me call over to the Poly Sci department, where Dr. Okapu had been a graduate student for eight years, to find out everything I could. It turned out that Dr. Okapu had survived a long dispute about whether his dissertation was passable, but he hadn't had a single job offer in the States and his visa had expired two years ago. Undocumented, he was living on mysterious means of support, but his three sons were very happy in the Greenglass schools.

"Think he's lying about the political stuff?" I wasn't sure whether I wanted Dr. Okapu to be a good guy or a bad guy. The dissertation had a chapter on Saro-Wiwa, written before the execution.

"I think we find out everything we can, to prepare for the hearing." Ted was a softie—well, you can guess who volunteers to work pro bono in the legal clinic—and he was going to put on the best show he could, no matter what I found out from Poly Sci. He just wanted to know the worst.

"If it took him eight years to get his doctorate, and then he stayed around without a green card another two, how could he have been helping Saro-Wiwa?"

"He went back a couple of summers. He has family in the region."

Something funny in his voice made me say: "Family?"

He gave me an even funnier look. "Another wife. And kids."

"Is he Muslim?"

Ted shrugged, and I didn't know whether that meant he'd divorced the other wife or not. Okapu would have been sent to this Catholic university from some other Catholic university, in Lagos probably, but I didn't have much of a sense of where the Ogonis came from or what religion they practiced—actually, I didn't have any sense of Nigeria, or Nigerians.

"He's not Muslim, he's just a lusty native." Ted said outrageous things about the clients all the time, especially Africans. He said *They'd lie about the time of day, if they knew what time of day it was*, and you had to remind him how maybe it wasn't such a great idea for an immigration lawyer to tell ethnic jokes about an entire continent which had, after all, fifty-four countries, and who knew how many cultures. If I did remind him, he'd pretend to laugh, but then he'd avoid me for days. I knew what he was thinking, though, because Frank used to say: *Don't be such a Puritan, Peg, can't you take a joke.* "Maybe you want to let Cornelia take this one off your hands?"

I didn't like the way Ted had been lingering at her desk lately, getting a good look at those plummy breasts. "Ah no. I find Dr. Okapu intriguing."

"That's good, because we're going to be seeing a lot of him."

* * *

And in fact, before the week was over Dr. Okapu returned with one of his sons, impossibly tall for such a tiny father. The boy, Winston, looked sixteen or seventeen. He wore short, fat dreads stuck up all over his head, a discreet gold cross in his ear, a tight, black leather jacket, enormous pants that drooped from his waist and flared along the floor, picking up dust. He didn't say a word, but he didn't hang back either. His eyes darted, taking in everything.

"Awesome jacket," Cornelia told him.

He flashed a golden smile. I was standing in the doorway to my office, gossiping with Dawn during the mid-afternoon slump. That week we'd had a dozen food stamps denials, five gas deposits required of single mothers who couldn't possibly pay, one vehicular homicide, a contested commitment to the state hospital, and three cases of domestic violence, including one in which a woman smashed her boyfriend over the head with an iron skillet that sprayed hot bacon fat over both of them. A father and son from a stable family, even it wasn't the only family the father had, made a pretty picture. I noticed that Dr. Okapu wore a black leather jacket too, though his floated above his chest.

Dawn said: "I'm sorry, Mr. Reilly's tied up in Chicago all day."

"We don't need Mr. Reilly personally." Dr. Okapu stood there.

"How can we help you?" Dawn was a patient matronly woman of sixty who had faced down loaded weapons. She looked the clients right in the eye, whether they were armed or not.

"I'm dropping Winston off."

"And how can we help Winston?"

Dr. Okapu looked at me as if all this were my fault. "Mr. Ted Reilly says he has an after-school job for him." His voice was sharp, higher-pitched than I remembered, the way he said *Mr. Ted Reilly* an accusation all by itself. I mistrusted him more than ever, but I tried to keep an open mind. Two years since the Ph.D. No job. Pricey leather jackets. And that other wife and family, back in Nigeria. Oh, my mind was wide open.

Dawn looked from Cornelia to me and back. "Hmmm. Mr. Reilly didn't mention anything about a job. Why don't you come tomorrow?" You could see her thinking *What in God's name is Ted thinking?* We had three interns floating through, Cornelia hogging the desk, no space to turn around. We needed more attorneys, not a sixteen-year-old boy who looked like an ad for the Gap.

Dr. Okapu said: "Mr. Reilly told me to come today."

Dawn said: "I don't know what we can do about that," and silence washed through the room like a wave. Dr. Okapu held his ground.

Finally Cornelia jumped in. "That's super you're working for us, Winston. Remember, Dawn? How Ted said we need somebody to messenger?"

She was right: the one thing we did need was a messenger, though we needed a plain old noun and not an infinitive. The clinic was a couple of blocks east of campus, on the raggedy edge of town. We moved it there so the people who needed our services wouldn't be intimidated, and it worked— now we had so many cases we were backed up for months—but the lawyers needed someone to deliver documents to campus or grab articles from the law library. Why they couldn't send Cornelia was a mystery, but I suppose it would have been beneath her sexy-young-wife-of-an-endowed-chair station.

Dawn got right in the spirit of things. "O happy day!" she sang. "I missed the pick-up and I was going to have to hike over there." She produced a Fed Ex envelope. "Do you know where the box is?"

Winston shook his head no while Dr. Okapu shook yes. He pinched at his son's elbow: "I'll drive you."

Dawn said: "Do you have a bike, Winston?" and we all looked down at his sagging pants. He laughed, easily, and Cornelia laughed with him.

"He hasn't had a bike since he was twelve years old," his father sniffed, as if a teenager on a bike was the most unseemly concept he had ever imagined, and Winston said the first words he'd spoken: "I'm a fast walker." He stuck his chin up in the air when he said it, just the way his father did, but his voice was low-pitched, self-assured. I liked him for it, liked him with such a rush of affection that I realized how much I missed having sixteen-year-old boys around, how much I needed someone with drooping pants in my life.

* * *

The entire first week, Winston stood by the door every afternoon, facing Cornelia's desk, silent and attentive as the clients came and went. They thought he was a security guard, an unforeseen benefit. We begged him to sit, but he said he couldn't take a seat the clients might need, and even when we scared up an extra chair he sat at attention, his spine straight. My opinion of Dr. Okapu, or at least of his child-rearing, rose. Sometimes when we had the office to ourselves Cornelia asked Winston for answers to the *Times* crossword puzzle—this kid who hoarded words was good with them—and sometimes she called him over to look at her computer screen. "Ooh, Winston, did you see about the Bulls?"

When she issued a summons, he rose slowly and went to stand behind her, neither stiff nor loose, waiting for her chatter to stop. Every now and again he flashed a wholly adult smile, as if he found her an amusing child. But she was flirting with him, and I didn't like it. He was sixteen years old. "Who did your hair this week, Winston? You ought to let me do it. I'd do it good. Um um." When he went out on a pick-up she said: "I feel badly for him."

"I feel bad," I muttered. I wasn't even sure she could hear me.

"I do, too. I feel so bad—" a long pause, as if maybe she'd finally figured out that I was correcting her—"the way he just sits here all the time."

"Well, you certainly keep him amused." My heart tightened like a fist.

After a minute she said she was just going out for a smoke. Glory be. I lived for these moments when she left, so I could talk to Dawn in private for a change, but Dawn looked me right in the eye and I knew that she had something to say.

"You have to go easy on her."

I played dumb. "You think I've been giving her a hard time?"

Dawn produced a tight smile to say I knew perfectly well what I was doing. It reminded me of the way she smiled ten years ago, when they gave me the promotion. I joked then that she'd finally have the whole reception area to herself, but we both knew that the difference between our paychecks would get a little bigger each passing year, her salary two inches over the poverty line. She'd been stuck in the secretarial pay grade forever, because she was so good at it.

But aside from that tight little smile she never held it against me. Once, when Frank was in the middle of leaving me, a client—a single mother, a large dark woman—went on a rampage in our office after her gas was cut off. "Look at these babies," she bellowed, "gonna freeze all night." I looked at the babies, bundled up on either side of her, and while I was looking she rose from her chair and threw it down in my direction. She herself was a bundle of flesh, her chins jiggling above a massive neck, charging toward me with her fists raised. Dawn was the one who hooked her by the elbow and told her that her behavior was completely inappropriate and called the gas company and got her on her way. I was nonfunctional through the whole thing. After the woman left, I tripped on the chair she'd overturned, and then I tripped on the doorjamb, going back into my own office. I let out a silly panicked cry. I must have sounded like a trapped animal, because Dawn said:

"What's wrong? Peg, what's wrong?"

I began to sob. "It's just too much. The refugees and the mothers with their gas bills, it's just too much."

Dawn came running and put her arm around my shoulder. "Oh, Peg. Oh, hon. It's not the lady with the gas bill you're crying for." I sniffled and she got a case of the giggles. "It's not the lady with the gas bill for whom you're crying."

We said, in unison: "Never end a sentence with a preposition," because we'd both learned our grammar from the Sisters of St. Joseph. It cracked us up.

"Frank says I'm uptight."

"Tell him to go soak his head in ginger ale."

"He says I only send out the urgent action appeals so I can pat myself on the back. That I only kept this job all these years so I could tell poor people what to do."

"Tell him to soak his head in motor oil."

"I don't know what to do. I don't know what to do about the clients or Frank or anything."

"You can only do what you do. One case at a time."

"At least I'm not rampaging through the office. Do I just want a pat on the back?"

She patted me on the back. "Some prisoner needs you to write a letter and you write it, and then you have to feel guilty too?"

I loved her for saying that. "I am wound a little tight."

"So what? If it keeps you doing what you have to do."

"I am a little controlling. A little judgmental."

She got the giggles again—twice in one day—and I told her I'd better hide at my desk because here came a client. But back in my office I began to cry again, and she let me, all afternoon, the Efficiency Queen weeping profusely at her desk, the clients staring in at me as if a madwoman had taken up residence. I felt I was sliding down a long dark chute. I tried to remember what the lady with the gas bill had looked like, but I could only see her chins, her neck, her bundles. At the end of the day Dawn brought me my coat and as she was handing it over she said: "Frank is an arrogant prick."

I'd never heard such a word from her lips. "I thought you liked Frank."

"Now you know." And now she said: "Mind if I go out there and have a smoke too?"

"Course not. I'll hold the fort." I was returning the little smile, I guess. All the secretaries smoked—there was nothing you could do about it—but since Cornelia came Dawn was up to a couple of packs a day. I wanted to tell her that I'd seen Cornelia scoop up two and three dollars in change from petty cash to go get her afternoon latté, that sometimes she called up her Victoria's Secret page on the screen all afternoon to torment Winston. My heart raced and my thoughts did, too.

The two of them were gone forever. They must have gone for a walk, or for coffee, or to talk over how I was abusing Cornelia. I heard Winston come back—I looked over my shoulder, to make sure it wasn't a client—and he saluted, a funny charming gesture. I saluted back.

But after a while I imagined he was standing in my doorway and when I looked over my shoulder again to reassure myself, there he was, standing in the doorway. I gasped, the way you do when somebody surprises you.

"Pretty scary, big black guy coming at you."

It was a joke. I laughed. "You don't scare me as much as some of the lawyers do."

He said: "That's what I wanted to ask you. You think my father has a shot at asylum?" It was the longest string of words I'd heard from him and he left me as speechless as his father had, that first day. Ted, who was usually so optimistic, had been hedging about the case.

"How old were you, when you came over?" I shouldn't have been asking him that. It didn't matter how old he was.

"Six."

"And your brothers? Were they born in Nigeria?"

"Yeah. I think they were, like, one and two when we got here. I know Buster cried the whole flight."

So Dr. Okapu brought three little children with him to America. And called his baby *Buster*. It probably would have been better if he'd just kept living below the radar, if he'd never filed for asylum.

"I don't want to go to Nigeria." Winston's eyes bore down on me. "I don't even remember what it's like. They execute people who protest there." *They execute...* Maybe he just knew how desperate I felt too sometimes, how my heart pounded so hard I thought it might fly away. Maybe that was why Winston Okapu stood in my doorway, asking me to perform some miracle.

* * *

The night Winston asked me to help him I went home and switched on the computer before I had a bite of dinner. I thought I could type in *Ken Saro-Wiwa* and finish up with my guilt—so much time had passed, nobody knew who he was—but page after page of Saro-Wiwa opened up to me. I'd never imagined a face to go along with my concept of the man, but there he was, a beaming man of fifty-four, the same age I was, sentenced to hang. Every photo showed him smiling, large perfect teeth gleaming under a jaunty mustache. In every shot he looked straight in the camera's eye. I couldn't bring myself to read about him—it was a judgment on me, on how I never lifted a finger to help—and when I put the computer to sleep I imagined it was haunted.

My night was haunted too. It wasn't just Ken Saro-Wiwa's face I saw in the dark. I dreamed the men who were executed with him, the ones who weren't famous, whose pictures never made it to the web. I counted Ogonis and Rwandans and Kosovars, mothers who couldn't pay the gas bill or the light bill or the rent. Their crowded faces floated above me in my lonely bed, too many, too many souls clamoring, speaking an English I couldn't understand. Dawn came to me in my twilight sleep—*One case at a time. One letter. Go easy, go easy, go easy*—and I drifted off for a little while.

But I couldn't stop my heart from pounding. The next day at work I got up and closed the door, as if I were about to leer at pornography, and typed in the name again. His story sprouted into electronic buds: Saro-Wiwa the novelist, the television producer, the activist. His last words to the court were inscribed on the screen, the way they might have been carved in stone a century ago. Random pieces of his life floated up at me: he sent five children to England for their schooling, but one of them had a heart condition and died, in the middle of a rugby match.

A rugby match. I imagined him in Nigeria, getting the call. Your son is dead, a continent away. Your son has collapsed on the field. Behind my closed door, my eyes filled, but this time I knew it wasn't Ken Saro-Wiwa I was crying for. It wasn't Saro-Wiwa for whom I was crying. I was crying for me, for my own sons, who'd gone off to lead their own lives. I was standing on the sidelines at their soccer games, the hot Greenglass sun beating down on the barren field. And when we got home I was berating their father, for insisting they play and then holing up in his office to work on his latest project. As soon as the youngest left for college—he went back East, the way his brothers had—Frank started a brand-new project, a tall assistant professor in fishnet stockings with breasts out to here. Our sons sobbed like babies over the phone when we told them and I could see the rest of my life rolling out with no one to hold in my arms, no one to touch. I felt good and sorry for myself. Right now, for all I knew, my boys were dating ambitious Wellesley girls who said *between you and I*. I could have taken the computer and heaved it through the window.

Only there was Ken Saro-Wiwa's smile on the screen. They arrested him, once, twice, and when he got out of jail he demonstrated all over again. They tried to kill him, and here he was. I was the one who was dead, the one whose vision was so narrow I'd never imagined a route out of this grim college town. I tried to picture a time when Frank had been tender to me, but I only remembered our boys making us pose for snapshots, his arm a log on my shoulder, my whole body flinching. Dawn was right: he was an arrogant prick. Why'd I pretend he'd broken my heart? And why—this came out of nowhere—why, if Winston's family were deported, couldn't I take Winston in? If I were in a big city I could say he was Rwandan, that I had adopted him. Nobody would think that was odd. My mind raced faster still. I tried to remember how many cups of coffee I'd had, how many hours of sleep.

A rap at my door. I started the way I did when Winston stood there. "Come in." I realized too late that I should have erased the screen.

Dr. Okapu stood in my doorway, and when I swiveled around, I was sure he could see Ken Saro-Wiwa smiling behind my chair. He didn't say a word about the computer screen, though. He gazed at a spot on the wall above my right shoulder. "No one is in this office."

"They've probably just gone out for a smoke."

"Where is my son?" He addressed me as if I'd kidnapped Winston.

"He must be on an errand, Dr. Okapu."

"Where is that . . . young woman? Who says her husband knows people in the State Department?"

"Cornelia?"

"I need to speak to her."

"Oh Dr. Okapu, does Ted know Cornelia's getting involved?"

"Ted!" He might have been spitting. "Mr. Ted Reilly has done nothing for us but get us deported."

"Deported? He hasn't said a word about that."

"How else can this end?"

We stared to the right of one another. Finally—I knew I shouldn't have said it, I knew it—I said: "Dr. Okapu, if you do go back to Nigeria, I could take Winston in."

Now he did spit, a slow sizzle through the gap in his front teeth. "Do you think I can't take care of my own sons?"

"No, Dr. Okapu, of course not."

"That I would hand them over? To—" He swept his arm across the room until it stopped at me. Then he pivoted on one heel and marched out. I heard him calling from the outer office: "Perhaps you would be good enough to ask Cornelia to call me."

* * *

Ted said the judge looked at Dr. Okapu, who was describing how he'd been photographed during a demonstration, as if he were a shifty-eyed drug dealer. "Which he was—well, the shifty-eyed part." Ted waited for me to tell him not to call a client *shifty-eyed*. "Why couldn't he just look the judge in the eye? If he wants to stay so bad." Still I didn't say anything. "So badly? If he wants to stay so much."

"Maybe it's a cultural thing. Not looking people in the eye."

"He damn well better learn that much about this culture." I'd never seen Ted that angry at a client: Dr. Okapu had shamed him in front of a big-deal federal judge.

"Will they be deported?"

"Well, you know . . ." What Ted meant was that the judge would deny asylum and issue a deportation order, but if Dr. Okapu really wanted to stay he could just disappear into the South Side of Chicago or even the West Side of Greenglass. He could get a new social security number for a thousand bucks, and Ted could probably tell him where to buy it—but he would always be looking over his shoulder.

"Do you think he really demonstrated with Saro-Wiwa?"

Ted was an attorney who knew better than to answer that question. He gave me a rueful smile and left for the Law School to teach his afternoon class.

I began to practice the blank faces I could wear when Winston came in after school.

"Bad news for the Okapu family?" I could have throttled Cornelia. Her husband was supposed to be *seeing what he could do*, but she probably hadn't even told him about the case. She strolled off in the afternoons with one intern or the other, and the petty cash box was always empty. And then when Winston came in an hour later, she let out a squeal for his new basketball jersey. "You made varsity!" He flashed his golden smile, went to his chair, sat at attention.

"Winston!" Cornelia wagged her finger. "Come let me give you a hug!"

He obeyed, slowly. She more than hugged him: she did a bump and a grind. I retreated to my office so I wouldn't say anything nasty, but from inside I could hear her carrying on: "You're going to have girls crawling all over you, Winston, you know you *are*. This is *super*. This is *awesome*. Varsity. Oh baby, I am proud of you. Are you going to let me do your hair now? Come on, let me braid you for the first home game, say you will."

I cleared my throat. The office settled down. But after a few minutes:

"Come look at this one. You should see me in this." I jumped to my feet and called her name. I would have dragged her into my office by the scruff of her neck if she had not come willingly. I met her halfway.

"Please close that door."

Showdown in the O.K. Legal Clinic Corral. We were six inches from each other. I could smell her Chanel. She was wearing a suit that might have been Chanel too, for all I knew, pink plaid over her curvy little hips.

"Cornelia, that boy is sixteen years old."

She looked at me as if I were mad.

"You have to stop tormenting him."

Now she was the one practicing blank faces. "I'm sorry if I did anything to offend you."

"To offend *me*?"

She scrunched the left side of her mouth. "Maybe you identify him with your own sons."

"This has nothing to do with me."

"Have you ever heard of projecting?" she said. "Because, you may not be aware of it, but white people do that—" She must have seen my face turning a floral shade of purple. I could hear my heart fluttering like a bird in my chest. "And also I think maybe you identify me with whomever busted up your marriage."

A little strangled cry left my throat. "*Who*ever busted up my marriage."

"I don't know who busted up your marriage. Just between you and I—"

I was calm at first, but in the chorus I heard myself picking up the pace. "You and me. You and me. You and me." I took a step forward. I slapped her in rhythm to my words, left cheek, right cheek, left cheek, right cheek. She was so surprised she let me, and I was so surprised I kept at it. I remember barking, "You steal the petty cash from a *poor people's clinic*," but Dawn says I said more, lots more, about stealing people's husbands and stealing young men's dignity. Dawn and I had a good giggle about it later, but right then I wasn't giggling. I had progressed to shaking Cornelia by the shoulders and evidently I was rattling her teeth, because when Dawn and Winston burst in they both looked frightened. They looked terrified. Cornelia was trying to push me away with her slender Chaneled wrists, so they peeled me off and Dawn pinned me against the wall.

"Just between you and *me*," I called to Cornelia, "I already know I'm uptight and judgmental and guilt-ridden. Ha!" I actually said *ha*. I was elated. It was all a big joke, though a joke on whom I'm not sure I could have said. Maybe I'd hit the bottom of the chute. I could finally remember what that lady with the gas bill looked like: above her chins a full mouth painted purple, a broad nose breathing fire. Her small eyes were wide-set, white-hot coals.

* * *

They offered me psychiatric help, but since I felt saner than I had in thirty years and said so, they had to let me go. After a couple of weeks, my heart slowed its fluttering and my mind didn't race as fast, so I called Ted to beg him to make Dawn the case manager. I was too late. Cornelia had already moved into my office.

But it turned out there were still a few months between the homeless shelter and me, so I took my time, figuring out where I was going and who I would be for the rest of my life. I didn't need to save Winston anymore. To everyone's surprise, the Okapus' asylum came through. Ted said somebody pretty high up in the State Department sent such a strong letter the judge didn't have a choice. Now Dr. Okapu actually had a green card, though he didn't have a job to go with it. He still sold leather jackets at a flea market on the outskirts of town, one of those places where green cards are as irrelevant as the provenance of the jackets. Dawn told me how to get there.

* * *

Under the low winter sky, shopping bags floating through the slushy parking lot, the place looked as depressed as the rest of Greenglass. A plastic yellow sign on wheels announced the latest load fallen off the truck. I recognized a Kosovar woman getting into her car: the mother of that kid who lost it in the middle school. People endured unspeakable sorrow and came all this way looking for a little peace, and instead they got this, cheap flimsy goods, imported just as we'd imported them.

I entered the long low shed and spied Dr. Okapu straightaway. He was wearing an old-fashioned fedora—a gray professor's hat—but he was playing the huckster, roaming the aisle in front of his stall, gesturing and putting his arm around a customer's shoulder. He looked taller in the hat. I still had no idea whether he was the good guy or the bad guy, but when I got close, I saw that he had framed a picture of Ken Saro-Wiwa for the back of his stall. In this dreary bazaar in this dreary town, Saro-Wiwa beamed down on me. I froze, but I made myself meet his smiling gaze, so full of life that you could imagine people all over the world remembering him and pulling up their socks, marching out to stop the oil companies and the gas companies and the military dictators. Beneath the picture, Dr. Okapu had set up a narrow table with two candles on it: a kind of an altar. He'd made a saint of Ken Saro-Wiwa and already I was doing the same, when the truth was, I didn't know any more about him than I knew about Dr. Okapu, or Nigeria, or Cornelia for that matter.

I waited till Dr. Okapu finished with his customer. When he spotted me, he nodded in that remote formal way of his, but then he relented and flashed a large gap-toothed smile. "You should read about this man. A great man. I can give you a book."

Did I take a step backward? No, his arm was around my shoulder, and I was trying not to flinch. "Thanks."

"I'm the one who owes you thanks," he said, in that unexpected high pitch. He thought I had something to do with the asylum.

"That was Cornelia who helped." It wasn't an easy sentence to choke out.

"Now, now, you mustn't be modest." He was a different man on his own territory, no longer at the mercy of lawyers and judges and case managers on the verge of nervous breakdowns.

"No really. I'm not responsible. I just came to ask if everything is OK with you and Winston. I . . . I think the world of him. He's a lovely boy."

"He is a good son." When he squeezed my shoulder, his eyes filled. He was a big mush—who would have guessed?

"Isn't there anything I can do for him? Anything I can do for you?"

Dr. Okapu let out a deep belly laugh, the first laugh I had ever heard from him. "Oh no no, my dear lady, I think we must agree that it's my turn now." He pressed me tight against his rib, and his laughter trailed off. "Isn't there anything I can do for *you?*"

THE OTHER WOMAN

IT TOOK SOME PEOPLE YEARS to see what was going on with the eighties, but I knew right from the beginning. I hated the eighties. I hated New York in the eighties. By the time she came after me, I'd already zoned into another time, another place.

I was walking down Seventh Avenue—this was Brooklyn, not Manhattan—and I got caught up in the crowd leaving the subway. I had forgotten about subways, about people piling out at rush hour. I'd given birth to my third child in June, and now it was the first week in August. There wasn't anybody left in New York in August, so what were all these people doing getting off the subway?

I was pushed along in the crush and I felt somebody stepping on my heels. That happens in a crowd on a narrow sidewalk. I hadn't been out without the children in so long that you might even say I was glad to have somebody stepping on my heels. I walked faster. After half a block, somebody clipped my left heel again and this time, I heard a woman's merry laugh. I turned around smiling, sure that the laugh was wrapped around an apology.

I didn't stop on the sidewalk—remember, there was a crowd surging along—but I got a good look at her just the same. She was tall, nearly as tall as I am, and she wore her straw colored hair shoulder length, like mine, with bangs—though hers were cut too short and pressed too flat to her forehead. Everyone in my family wears straw-colored hair and pale skin spattered with freckles; she might have been a Feeney. She even had something of a pot belly to match my postpartum swell. Her clothes were just awful—a pink floral shirt and matching stretch pants—but I was trying not to pay attention to clothes. In the eighties, that was all anybody talked about, that and their co-ops and their cheese and their restaurants. They weren't onto gardening yet.

I was right about one thing: she was merry, all right, just delighted that she'd stepped on me twice. Her face was round and doughy, pocked as if a fork had pricked holes, and wouldn't you know, that was just about how I was feeling about my face in the eighties. I hadn't gone on an audition since Gracie, the middle child.

I crossed the street, half expecting her to follow me, but she didn't. I told myself I was getting paranoid, but really I was excited to think that she did it on purpose. I had walked out, actually, hoping to catch a young man's eye—another out of work actor or a fireman buying groceries—but not a man saw me passing through the streets.

Back home, it took all my energy to climb the stairs. We lived on the top floor of a brownstone in a big sunny apartment with a fireplace and a dumb-waiter leading nowhere. I loved that apartment—it was a seventies place, still rented cheap—but Jean-Paul was ashamed of living in a walk-up. We went to look at co-ops every Sunday.

At the apartment door I could hear Helen switching off the television; she must have been the only adult woman still in Brooklyn in August, besides me and my doppelgänger. Inside, it was close to ninety degrees, unless you were standing right beside one of the fans. All three children were asleep, just as I'd left them, burning with fever. The sun beat down on the flat tar of the roof all day, and they couldn't shake this bug.

Helen stood by the television, glad to be caught. She was a gaunt woman with wattles, maybe forty, maybe fifty. She'd been crying.

"Did you hear about that new disease?"

I thought she had a theory about the kids' viruses. "What disease?"

"AIDS. You read about that?"

I nodded. It was only a few months old then; rather, it was only a few months since we all knew about it.

"My brother's got AIDS, but it's not what you think. He's a junkie."

I thought about putting my arms around her, but she stepped back, as if she sensed what was on my mind. "Now you probably don't want me to use the toilet. Or watch the kids at all."

Not want Helen to watch the kids? The whole world was in Martha's Vineyard or the Hamptons, or even, if they were renters like us, in some little North Carolina beach town. We were still in the city because we had a new baby and our children were sick and Jean-Paul thought a vacation not taken would count for a lot at bonus time.

Maybe we were still there because of this woman he was seeing. He hadn't said anything about a woman, but I sensed her in every room of the apartment: we lived with her cool slender presence. She was chic and childless. She came from money and she made her own money, too. She was there in his irritation with the apartment, with my clothes, with the babies always sick. He wanted to say something, too, to confess. He came home very late and hung his head down and stared out into dark space. His grandfather wouldn't have thought anything about having affairs, but Jean-Paul was first-generation, American enough to crave the guilt.

It was so hot. Just don't tell me about it, I used to think. I was too tired. I couldn't remember loving him, though I must have once, and not too long before. Three babies. He was very handsome, with thick black curly hair that he'd cut short for the eighties. He still looked good, very French movie star, in his little black bikini when we went to Jones Beach. But he hated going to a public beach and dragging home sand in the car, so we hadn't gone together in a long time. I drove out there alone, with the babies, when no one was running a fever.

* * *

Helen was hard to get, now that she spent so much time with her brother in the hospital, and often when she was able to come I had no plans in mind, just a need to walk the streets alone. One day I found myself making broad circles of the neighborhood, up to Prospect Park, down to Seventh Avenue. Finally I went in a daze to the cash machine, just to look at the balance, to see if finally having enough money made me feel better or worse.

The air conditioning in the bank lobby steadied me. I put my card in the slot and punched in Jean-Paul's code—the words *red wine*—but I never saw the figures come up on the screen. From behind me, she put her hands over my eyes, the way kids do in the schoolyard. Her fingers were small and cool, though it was ninety-five outside the bank's inscrutable dark window. My own palms were streaming sweat. For a millisecond I tried to persuade myself that it was one of the other neighborhood mothers, back early from the Cape or Maine, but she pressed her fingers hard against my eyelids, and I knew for sure. My friend from the crowd.

When I pried her hands loose and swung around to face her, she grinned, and then she gave me a little slap on the cheek, a gentle slap. Playful. She had her hair pulled back in a ponytail and so did I. I could see from her gray eyes, not quite focused, not quite engaged, that she was on heavy medication. There was a group home up near the park.

She was there, and then she wasn't there. She skipped off the way the schoolgirl who'd covered my eyes might have done, and the bank door swung shut in rhythm with my eyes blinking. Now that she was gone, I felt a clutch of fear, and my milk let down in a gush. I walked home with my blouse soaked through, and still the firemen, buying their groceries at the Key Food, looked right over me and around me and through me, as if I weren't there at all.

By the time I let myself in upstairs, the milk had dried sour on my shirt. Helen met me at the door, holding the baby as if he were already a little corpse. "In the space of an hour," she said. "A hundred and four."

"He's two months old. Babies don't run fevers like that. They've been fine all week."

"I was just waiting for the car service. Your doctor said get him down to emergency, there's meningitis all over the city."

* * *

They did a spinal tap—they made me wait outside the door, so I wouldn't run to Gabe when he screamed—but he didn't have meningitis. Jean-Paul showed up just as it was all over. He looked so capable in his new linen suit that I wanted to burrow my face in his chest. I was still imagining the baby's gasp of betrayal when they dug the needle into his spine.

"My God," Jean-Paul said, once he heard Gabe was all right. "What is that on the front of your blouse?"

* * *

Everything was feverish in the eighties. Our neighbor was knifed in the ribs, walking home from work at seven o'clock, and everyone on the block talked about moving to Jersey or the Hudson River Valley, but he was released from the hospital after one day, and we all stayed put.

One night I looked down from the living room window and saw two guys bent over, one almost atop the other. I thought it was another mugging. From the fourth floor, the two figures were shadows, their arms and heads a twilight color that did not define their races. I opened the window to see better, to yell down, and when they heard my *Hey* we all froze. Is that the right word, *froze*, if you're in a fever?

Stretching out the window, I could see that this was no mugging, that they were kids leaning into our car, stealing our battery—we'd already lost one battery and the hubcaps and the rear window—and I had the urge to leap down to the sidewalk. I wanted to grab them by the ears, little boys that they were, and make them look me in the eye.

I was glad that I couldn't see what race they were in the evening light. Jean-Paul's dark-skinned family was from Marseilles. He liked to speculate what blood might have mixed with the French: African, Portuguese, Arab? My family was terrified by his darkness. My oldest, Paul, was also dark. I'd seen people look from him to me and back. The neighborhood was integrated when we moved in, but by the eighties it seemed very white. I began to dislike white people. I had no doubt that they would eye my Paul on the street when he was a teenager, that they would wait for him to stick a knife in their ribs. I began to see all white people as pale freckled Feeneys telling me to move back to their safe enclaves on Long Island. I was sick of their guessing my own fear. You saw these kids on television in the eighties, their eyes not so much vacant as switched off, not so much defiant as mocking. Some reporter in a short skirt, stroking a microphone, asked them what they thought about when they knocked old people down and they snickered.

I'd heard men on our block talk about beating the shit out of the kids who stole their hubcaps and their batteries and their trim. They talked about beating the kids who, when they weren't too stoned, figured out how to take the whole car.

* * *

The night after I saw them disconnecting the battery, they got the whole car. Jean-Paul was delighted, because now he could get a Saab or a Peugeot, but we had to wait a month for the insurance money. The last month of summer. The children's fevers had dwindled, leaving their faces pinched and pasty, but now I couldn't drive them to Jones Beach. So instead I loaded down the stroller and Paul and Gracie's backpacks and trundled them onto the D train for Brighton Beach.

Jean-Paul thought it was madness. Used condoms littered the sand and every once in a while you'd see a hypodermic—the hospital waste washing up—but at least there were no crack vials yet. This was only '83, remember. I was so glad to be with my babies, walking on the boardwalk, that there could have been dead bodies on the beach and it wouldn't have fazed me. When we were acting students, Jean-Paul bought me a poster of Coney Island, the Weegee photograph. Maybe you know it: a beachful of bodies, immigrant bodies, stretching back for miles, almost as many people as grains of sand on that beach. I always imagined there were Feeneys there, straight over from County Kerry. They're all happy, silly, mugging for the camera.

As August wore on, I took the children to Brighton Beach or Coney Island every day. After a week my pale friend learned our route and trailed us up Seventh Avenue to the D train. The children didn't deter her in the least. Paul and Gracie were all over the sidewalk, dragging sticks usually, so she sneaked around them to give me a soft punch in the shoulder or tug my hair or stick her tongue out. It was a scary tongue—short and fat and coated the same yellow as a Brooklyn morning—but only Paul was old enough to be scared. Gracie loved it when our friend made an appearance; she clambered into the back of the stroller, and I grabbed Paul's hand, and we all took off to catch her. She was quick disappearing into stores, around corners, and Paul's little legs never held out for more than a block or so. Once, though, we followed her all the way home, to a big limestone in a park block, the kind of house bankers and brokers live in, a gracious house with big bowed windows and a sweet old-fashioned front garden of pansies and petunias. She raced up the stoop and slipped behind the front door. "Go," Gracie whispered from the stroller. "Go."

It was the halfway house for chronic mental patients. We parked on the sidewalk, my children and I, and watched the front windows, roman shades drawn halfway. Roman shades—that's my picture of the eighties—but I had never expected to see them hanging halfway in a halfway house. The children and I giggled, waiting for her to show her face. It gave her so much pleasure to follow me on the street, to make physical contact, that the pleasure became contagious. I remembered her merry laugh that first day she tripped me. This house looked merry, too. This was the city I wanted, a city crowded with group homes and yellow flowers and immigrants mugging for the camera.

The children got tired of waiting. She never showed herself or peeked out, and finally I walked back home, the beach bags dragging off the stroller. The sun beat down through a Brooklyn haze. Fatigue overtook me. Suddenly I could not bear the thought of Brighton Beach, of leaving dirty diapers balanced on overflowing garbage cans. I couldn't bear the thought of one more drunken man exposing himself to me. Gracie wept, because we were not going to the beach after all, and Paul, as we trudged up our own front stoop, asked me if I thought we could have imagined that woman who followed us all the time. That was the eighties: even children couldn't tell what was real.

* * *

Jean-Paul came home at dusk one night and said he had to speak to me, now, before I put Gabe to bed. I held the baby close, a shield against what I knew was coming, but Jean-Paul looked ferocious. I lay Gabe down in his cradle and left Paul and Gracie watching *Sleeping Beauty*. They'd developed a special fondness for witches.

We made our way down the narrow brownstone hall and sat stiffly in the living room. Just don't say it, I thought. Just don't tell me.

"I've been so depressed," he said.

I stared out the window. The sky was darkening fast, and on our leafy block the streetlights were dim.

"I've been seeing someone."

Don't say it. Don't say it.

"She charges ninety-five an hour but I think it's worth it."

I thought he was telling me how much he paid a call girl—really I did—and a funny squirting sound left my mouth.

"She's talking about a prescription, but I think I can stay off meds . . ."

A shrink. When we were all actors, no one could afford a shrink; now I was the only one I knew without one. But I was sure he'd been having an affair. He couldn't bear to brush up against me. In the heat of an August night, when I lay alone in bed crazy with wanting, he sat on the fire escape until he was sure I was asleep. Maybe this was only the first part; maybe I would have to wait for months until he had the courage to tell me the rest of the news. I was so tired. The stoop was so steep. Gabe woke three and four times a night. No one would be home until after Labor Day.

"Oh Jean-Paul. It's all right. Just go ahead and leave."

"Do you think I would leave you," he said, "with three little children?"

His words, his sense of obligation, chilled me. I rose slowly and walked back down the narrow hallway. My shoulder bag hung over the doorknob. I heaved it up and walked out of the apartment, down the three flights of stairs, down the long stoop, out into the gray Brooklyn night. The air was heavy and still.

I was chilled and I was in a fever. I walked to the cash machine, past the barrels of stinking garbage, and I withdrew the maximum. I would have a car service take me to Manhattan. I would spend the night in a hotel. I would call Jean-Paul and tell him where I kept the emergency formula. In the morning I would gather my babies up and retreat to the Feeneys on Long Island. They were the only ones who would have me.

But first, I needed to walk by the group house one last time. I needed to see if my stalker spent her nights staring out the windows the way I did. I walked along the avenue, past the new restaurants and the little stores I didn't recognize anymore. The owners turned over every six months in the eighties, because they all thought they could afford the rent and they couldn't. This wasn't their place and it wasn't my place anymore, either.

I turned toward the park. I should have felt light without the stroller, without the babies, but all my muscles strained. I heard footsteps behind me and looked over my shoulder: a couple licking white ice cream off each other's cones. They opened a garden gate and turned in.

I reached the park block alone, but as I started up I heard footsteps again. I crossed the street so that I could get a good look and she crossed, too, behind me. My friend. If it hadn't been darkening so quickly, if the street hadn't been so lonely, maybe we would have been merry. But she was striding along, hellbent, and I braced myself.

My milk let down again. My hair was loose tonight. A tug of the hair, a punch in the shoulder: what was I so worried about? I knew her pretty well by now. I found myself thinking that I shouldn't have turned away from Jean-Paul. I walked uphill, toward the park, the pad of her sneakered feet gaining on me. Go ahead, do your worst. We walked along in single file, the pair of us. At the top of the block, faces peered around the big apartment building at the corner. Kids.

They saw me see them—maybe they couldn't see her behind me—and they made their move. They came down the block together, five boys, four of them large, their pants slipping down their waists, the bills of their baseball caps bobbing in the night. Goony birds. I moved to walk in the street—even suburban Feeneys know to do that—but as I veered off the sidewalk they split up, three marching to the opposite sidewalk, two staying behind on mine. There was no point to walking in the middle of the street. My breath was short, my thighs trembling. They played a game in the eighties, knocking people down with a single blow.

One boy followed the other. I tried to make eye contact with the first, the shortest of them. When I saw him glance sidewise, I knew I'd pass him safely. Something flickered in his face—not guilt, just something. The second boy kept his face averted. He was the one. As we passed he reached his right fist across my body and struck me in the mouth.

My breath came long and easy then. Now that it was real, I wasn't afraid. The five boys crowded me, pummeling, grabbing for the strap of my bag. I was in a barroom brawl. I was facing down Jean-Paul's lover. I spat in one face, then another. Later, people on the block told me that I was screaming holy hell. Actually, they said I screamed: *Look at me. Look at me.* They thought there was a crazy woman loose.

But I didn't know that I was screaming. I could feel my fists flailing, my shoes making contact with shins. A large hand grabbed my foot, and then I was flat on my back. They pulled me to the gutter, between two cars, the smell of shit close to my face. Maybe they would drag me to the park. They leaned over, crowding, pushing each other back, and I memorized each boy's dark face as it hovered. The smallest boy had a high forehead, a nose as long and broad as Jean-Paul's, light eyes: startled, startling. His thick lashes might have been my Paul's.

From above I heard windows raised, ineffectual voices calling down: *Hey. Hey!*

The jellied mass of them hesitated, wavering. I was on my feet again, fists windmilling. When they turned to run, together, as if on cue, I thought I had defeated them single-handedly. Not bad: one against five. Still drunk on adrenaline, I took off after them. I would follow them into the park as they scattered. I would track one of them down, the one with the startled eyes. I would make him look at me.

I heard the police car behind me grinding up from the bottom of the block. I counted the bodies ahead—how many had escaped?—and saw that where there had been five boys running, there were now six figures in front of me. One of them had long straw-colored hair. The siren came closer. The bodies ahead ran uphill into the night.

She managed to hold one of them at the corner. By now the police lights flashed at my shoulder, but I didn't look their way. It didn't seem real anymore, and I stumbled. Under the streetlight, my crazy friend held the boy by one arm, pulled behind his back, and by one ear. She twisted it, the way the nuns used to do our ears, so that he would have to look at me as I drew near. It was the smallest boy, the boy with the light eyes. Under the streetlamp, I could see that they were green. He shifted them back and forth.

I would make him look at me, and maybe I would take his other ear and give it a good twist. I would make him look, and I would get a good long look at him. I should not have turned away from Jean-Paul.

She must have been strong to hold a kid, sixteen or seventeen, muscular, sullen. He held his face impassive, the eyes still darting. The two police car doors slammed shut in unison. My stalker grinned and stuck her yellow tongue out at me. We all had so much to answer for in the eighties. I stuck my own tongue out, happy. I was mugging for the camera, jostling in a crowd, zoning into some other time, some other place.

THE AGE OF INFIDELITY

I WASN'T BUT SEVEN WHEN Holly drowned in the river, so I spent my childhood chasing a vision. She was nine years older: sweet sixteen when she died in the summer of 1960, boyfriends tying up the party line night and day and no wonder. She wore crinolines, two or three at least beneath her swirling skirt, and pulled her dark hair back in a poof, with curled-under bangs to balance. Did she go dancing in saddle shoes? We only had the one school picture of her on the mantel, all the others packed away, so I got my ideas about what she should wear from re-runs of *Dobie Gillis,* Holly's favorite show. And maybe I had to strain to remember what she looked like, but the funny thing was: I could hear her just fine. I could hear her cajoling my mother, clear as if they were both standing over me.

Can I go out on the river?

MAY *I go out on the river.*

All right. May *I go out on the river.*

No, you may not. I do not trust a teenage boy with a boat.

You are the meanest woman ever walked the earth.

Holly's voice was soft and fluty, bored, and if she used it to drive my mother crazy, my mother always got her revenge by bellowing *no,* in a voice like a bassoon, to whatever Holly asked. When she was doing well enough to sing without disrupting the entire choir, my mother was the clearest deepest alto at Division Street Methodist.

She kept up the choir after Holly died, kept up most everything and seemed to be doing as well as anybody could expect of a mother who'd lost half her children, till one day I came from school to find her crouching in the hallway. It was three years since Holly died. She wouldn't get up off her haunches till I'd closed all the drapes against the gunman she saw on the roof across the way. He'd been watching her for hours, waiting to pick her off. She got the idea from Lee Harvey Oswald, so I guess you could say we were both taking our visions off the TV set.

* * *

That first time my mother was up in the state hospital close on to a year and I wasn't allowed to visit, so naturally I pictured her in a damp dungeon with chains around her ankles. My father came back from seeing her with his face gone as gray-green as modeling clay. I figured out I should probably be cooking for him and found my mother's *Lowcountry Receipts*. When she was home we didn't eat anything out of the river, but I got to be pretty good with deviled crab and boiled shrimp, which my father ate like he was scared the ocean might run out. We set down two big plates of shrimp on newspaper, a bowl of melted butter between us, and that was all we needed in the world. On the nights he was home, we made ourselves comfy with the television, which my mother hated. We took to watching the news during supper, and after the news something to make us laugh.

When she was finally discharged, her voice muffled so you could hardly understand her, we stopped buying seafood at the docks and we thought we'd have to turn the TV off, too. But when my father was out she sat right down with me and watched with a puzzled look on her face, as if everybody onscreen was speaking Hungarian. That I should like *That Was the Week That Was* was beyond human comprehension, or her comprehension anyway.

"I don't believe I can live this way."

She waited till my father left to hide her pills and to show me just which shelf they would be sitting on in case of emergency. She said that with the help of Jesus she was going to practice mind control and after a week, sure enough, she smiled at the television. After two weeks she laughed till the tears streamed down. After three weeks she was completely herself and it was just like the old days:

"What are we doing wasting our lives on television? Why was it ever invented."

Then it was time to paint the master bedroom and re-line the linen closet and why not move the garage door while we were at it. She could sleep for three days straight after she'd been on a rampage. We went back to ham and chicken, no more crab or shrimp or anything else that might smell of the river.

You have to understand, when you talk about the river in Due East you could be talking about a marsh or a creek or the bay or the sound, all of them tidal, salty, clumped through with marshgrass, meandering till they flow into one another. The currents are crazy. When a boy says *Do you want to go out on the river* he means get in his Boston Whaler or his Sailfish or, if he's rich, his catamaran. He means go where the water takes you, and that might be as far as the ocean. When I turned sixteen I heard an echo: Holly, begging to go out on the river, and my mother denying her.

Everybody in this whole town, everybody in this whole entire town.

You are not everybody. Those currents are treacherous.

Oh Mama, for goodness sake. Life's treacherous.

I would never in a million years say that life was treacherous or ask if I could go out on the river. It was a word we didn't say in our house, like the word *crazy,* or the word *dead,* a story we didn't tell. I still didn't know whether Holly fell off the boat or jumped or a storm came up fast or who knew what all. It even occurred to me that somebody might have pushed her. She could swim, I knew that much. I knew because our mother said why take swimming lessons, what good did they do Holly, they only made her think she could go out on the river and play Russian Roulette with her life.

See how I called her *our mother* instead of *my mother?* She'd been practicing her mind control for six whole years and she was hellbent on controlling me too. I needed Holly's backtalk in my ear.

"May I go to the show Friday night please?"

"With whom?"

"With Jack."

"And who might I ask is Jack."

"You know. Jack Wesley."

"I don't believe I approve of that name for a Methodist child."

"Jeez louise, his name is homage."

"Language!"

"But he's named in *honor* of John Wesley."

"Who will be driving?"

"Jack."

"Does he have his night license."

"Yes ma'am."

"Is the car equipped with seatbelts."

"No, Mama. Aw come *on.*" "Well, why doesn't his car have them."

"He's got an old Studebaker from when they hadn't even invented seatbelts."

"You're not going anywhere in an old Studebaker. My word."

"No, I'm not going anywhere ever but just stay locked up in this house forever."

"You may go out with Jack when he finds a newer more appropriate vehicle equipped with seat belts."

You are probably thinking: naturally she felt that way. She lost one daughter, she was not about to lose two. But she was the same about watching *Laugh-In* or *I Spy* or playing a record by the Kinks. The Kinks! And no, I could not go to some ecumenical service, we knew who we were. WE KNEW WHO WE WERE. Next thing I'd be asking to go to Mt. Zion A.M.E., or maybe I'd like Temple Beth Israel better than Division Street Methodist.

She confiscated my *Revolver*. No I couldn't go to Merilee's beach house, and no I couldn't go to a movie if it starred that homewrecker Elizabeth Taylor. Not five minutes after she said her last *no*, she was humming "Love Divine, All Loves Excelling," or "Blest Be the Dear Uniting Love," while she rearranged the spice rack in alphabetical order, her face set smug and victorious.

* * *

She caught me by surprise when she showed up at the high school and got them to call me down to the office in the middle of French class. You only heard your name called over the intercom for a family tragedy and truth to tell, I was pretty sure my father had killed himself. What put such an idea in my head I cannot to this day tell you, but that was my fear when I came into the office at a full gallop. My mother spun around from the front desk to face me, index finger to her lips, signaling me to hush. This was our little secret.

Out in the hallway I took her by the elbow and steered her through the front door before she got me in any worse trouble with her tittering. If you've ever heard a woman with a voice like a bassoon titter, you know that it is a dislocating sound.

"What's wrong? What's wrong."

"Not a thing in the world, lambkin. I'm stealing you away to the bazaar."

"What bazaar?"

She gave me a look. Due East had only two bazaars a year, Catholic in the fall and Episcopal in the spring, and the buds had already opened on all the magnolia trees. Why did she want to go their bazaar? Episcopalians were a tad too lax about their faith for my mother's taste and then, she always said, there was the false friendship. They'd ask you in for a cup of tea and they'd start to talk about the latest books and before you knew it you felt small, which was their intention all along.

Why don't you read the latest books then.

I would never say such a thing aloud to a woman practicing mind control with the help of Jesus. Before she got married my mother lived with all the other single women at the teacherage and taught French at the junior high, and learned to speak the way teachers do, turning questions into sentences so you know exactly who's in charge. She was from the upcountry, the first person in her family to make it all the way through high school, much less college. Her people were lintheads who worked the textile mills, their accents so thick you couldn't understand a word they said unless you grew up among them. In college, she said, she learned how to speak two new languages, not just French but the English she'd never heard properly spoken before. If she was going to teach me anything, it was how to speak so I didn't shame myself, but what I learned from her was how to turn my questions into sentences.

"Mama what do you think you're doing. I'm in the middle of French class."

"You can go to school any old day of the week."

"You're the one said I had to take French."

"It will change your life! You'll travel the world the way I would have done."

"You won't even let me out the house."

"Didn't I just take you out of school. And fib to do it."

"Mama I think maybe you better take one of your pills."

"Oh fiddle-dee-dee."

I knew we were in big trouble when she started doing her Scarlett O'Hara. People were supposed to think they were Jesus or Satan when they went nuts, not Vivien Leigh. She skipped along to her car, waiting for us in the No Parking zone, and slid behind the wheel. She said she'd be my French teacher for the day and commenced to conjugate simple verbs she could still remember, *chanter* and *s'amuser*, only they sounded like *chanteye* and *samooz-eye* in her upcountry accent. She said she would have gone to Paris if she hadn't married my father, but they would have laughed us both out of Paris.

She thought she was driving stylishly, weaving through cars on the John C. Calhoun Road. She forgot she had a blinker, much less a seat belt. When she got to the Episcopal Church all the other big sedans were angled willy-nilly by the side of the street, but she decided to parallel park and in one swoop she parallel parked herself right into the back of a fat live oak. We heard a taillight crunch.

"Ça ne fait rien. We'll think about that later."

"Mama, maybe we better drop by the house first and pick up those pills."

"Oh sweetheart sugar, poor lamb. Those pills are dust."

She gave me a sad quiet look, as if she pitied me for all I had to learn about the world. She was right. Those pills were old, and it wasn't like we could go show up at my father's insurance agency either, not after all the trouble my mother had already given his secretary. No, it was just me between my mother and the nuthouse.

I followed her down the brick path through the old crumbling tombstones. She sniffed at the blooms just opening and said she'd never seen the attraction of white roses herself. At the door to the parish house, she shrank back a little. She was used to Methodist ladies, who mostly looked just like her, their hair dyed a shiny bright shade and their fingernails like scarlet talons. Episcopalians, now. They let their hair grow out white and twisted it back with bobby pins, and they wore flats instead of high heels, and they tootled off to Paris anytime they liked. I peeked in over my mother's shoulder and saw the first room of the bazaar, where they laid out all the linens, the embroidered napkins, the crocheted doilies, the needlepoint pillows. Over in the back corner they had watercolors propped up on easels but I knew we'd never get to the paintings, or to the rooms beyond where you could guess how many painted peach pits in the pot or date the arrowhead. I could feel my mother's whole body tremble.

"Ooh! Isn't that darling."

She scooped up an armful of linen at every table she passed. Piles of material unfolded at her feet and cotton dust flew around her head. She stopped at one table to finger the scalloped hems, at the next to ogle the white roses embroidered on pillowslips. I guess she could see their attraction better in here. When she clicked open her pocketbook, bills fluttered to the table below, and white-haired ladies scooped them up. They didn't even look like they thought she was crazy—they were too polite for that—but still I held up her load of tea towels so they couldn't see my face.

"My goodness gracious. I have got to have that one."

She dashed over to pick up the most unEpiscopalian pillow I ever hope to see, a portrait of Jesus just as gaudy as a portrait of Elvis, pink on a purple background. His blond hair and beard flowed out in ringlets till he looked like a white rose himself.

"How much is that?"

"Isn't that something?" said the Episcopalian lady.

"How did you make such a thing?"

"Mercy! I didn't make it," laughed the lady. "Is it worth seven dollars to you?"

"Oh dear Holly, do we have that much left?"

"I can see you've been on a little spending spree," the lady said.

"Yes we have. Holly and I have decided to live a little today."

"We've even decided to raise the dead." I didn't have to say that last, I know it was uncalled for, but my mother didn't even know she'd called me by my dead sister's name. She didn't know anything she was doing, not that she held twenty sheets in her arms or that she'd spent all my father's money. She might just as well have guzzled down a bottle of Episcopalian sherry and walked through their bazaar stark naked. And they would have been just as pleasant.

"Isn't it a comfort to have your daughter's help?"

"Yes, indeed. Ma petite fille reste dans le tiroir."

"I beg your pardon?"

But my mother had run out of words, and stared at the lady with the same incomprehension that used to visit her when she was watching TV. Finally it occurred to her to say:

"What's the name of this church? Notre Dame? Sacré Coeur? Au secours?"

A look of panic crossed her eyes. She didn't even know what country she was in, or how to tell people you were loony tunes. The lady too wore a puzzled troubled look but she held out her own trembling hand for my mother to grab hold.

She made a dash for it instead. The pile of bed sheets in her arms began to topple off, and soon enough she was on her knees, grabbing for what she'd lost. The Episcopalian ladies all ventured out from behind their tables, hands to their mouths. Some of them called for help, in plain old English anybody could understand.

* * *

Naturally she had to go up to the state hospital again, and this time I was old enough to visit. The sight of the heavy gray metal lock-door she lived beyond chilled me like nothing I have ever seen before or since. It took forever for someone to come let us in, and that someone was a perky little redhead of a nurse, the kind to make me puke.

"Hey there, Mr. Matthews. I see you brought your daughter to visit! Now isn't that going to do Miz Matthews a world of good."

"Is she in her room?"

"I'm afraid she's in the quiet room just now."

"Oh dear. She didn't."

"No, she didn't hurt anybody."

"Oh no. Should we—"

"You just come by the TV and I'll find an orderly, see if she's calmed down some. Does she ever speak in tongues?"

"No, I don't believe so. We're just plain old Methodists."

"You hang onto that sense of humor. You're going to need it!"

We walked down a long dark corridor shot through with dust motes. Patients shuffled along behind us like they were crippled or shackled. We passed the nurses' counter and headed toward a big TV mounted from the ceiling, a dozen plastic chairs scattered beneath it. One little old lady sat hunched over. I couldn't tell if she was white or black, her skin that pecan shade that might come from working all your life in the hot sun or might come from mixed up genes. She held her face down so low we couldn't see her properly.

We sat down next to her and presently we saw that she was watching an interview with some Marine who looked even younger than I did. The Marine said lately they'd been throwing Viet Cong from helicopters. He'd seen them do it, he'd done it himself, it made him sick. He had to tell someone. He told how they hogtied the Cong and put them in the chopper and threw them into the sea. It was like all those years ago when Jack Ruby shot Lee Harvey Oswald right in front of us and we couldn't stop it happening and we couldn't stop them showing us. They told us over and over again what we'd just seen, as if otherwise we would never understand. They had my mother in a straitjacket. I felt my own arms tied back. The old lady mental patient was making twitchy motions with her hands and feet.

"I be hearing things again."

"No ma'am, you're not imagining."

"Child, you wouldn't lie to me?"

"No ma'am," I said, the way I'd been taught to do. "It's the gospel truth."

"That soldier lying? All that evildoing?"

My father said, "I sure to God hope so. Let me see if I can shut this thing off."

"Oh, they won't let you shut it off. No sir. You got to sit and take it."

My father rose and took a step toward the TV, but it was high above him and no nurses in sight. I guess they could get away from bad news all right. He sat back down. Mental patients, some of them dressed and some of them in pajamas and some of them half-and-half, came to look us over. Sometimes they snorted or shook their heads like we weren't at all who we were supposed to be. My father jumped up to light one man's cigarette when the lighter glued to the wall didn't work. I didn't even know he kept matches in his pocket. Five minutes passed, ten minutes, fifteen. I couldn't swallow. I got some phlegm up from the back of my throat and then I couldn't breathe. I was drowning sure as Holly drowned. My arms were tied behind me. I was drowning sure as those Viet Cong.

"Daddy I can't . . ."

At the sound of my voice he turned to face me and I saw that he'd gone that gray-green color and would rather not hear any more trouble: one daughter dead, who knew how, and one wife crazy. I was just going to have to sit and take it.

"Look! Here she comes."

And there was my mother shuffling down the hall wearing her white nightie, escorted by an orderly who looked for all the world like a prison guard. From where we were sitting in the television's glow we could see a lopsided grin on her face, as if she knew she'd been a very naughty girl. My father leaned in close and said:

"You know, her people were fearful generally. She can't get past that."

His speech took me by surprise. I told him I understood how Holly made her crazy, but he said, "No, honey, she was sick before. I've been dealing with this a long, long time."

I hadn't heard him say something so important in sixteen years, but here she was already, looming above us with her guard at her elbow. We sat there stuck to our TV chairs. My father didn't even say hello. Her hair was beginning to grow out gray at the temples. I could see through her white nightie to her nipples, brown circles as big as silver dollars. Wouldn't you think they'd put a robe on her?

But she was just as cheerful as she could be. She was just a giggly girl again when she looked my father right in the eye and said:

"Is my little girl cooking you all that seafood you like? Has she moved into our bedroom yet? Has she moved into our bed?"

I'll ask you: do you think you could ever forgive your mother, she said something like that? I'd never heard anything so disgusting in all my days. I wouldn't go back to visit, not once, and I blamed her entirely for the dreams I was having, when I threw her out of a helicopter and sometimes threw the red-headed nurse behind her for good measure.

This time she wasn't gone nearly so long, and when she came home she waltzed in as if that conversation had never happened. She shut the news off and she served us heavy roasts, all she had the concentration to fix, just when we were starting to savor oysters again. I couldn't so much as meet my father's eye if she was in the same room. I couldn't meet his eye whether she was in the room or not.

This time my father stood over her to make sure she took her pills and she swallowed them down like communion. Her tongue was thick, as if it had swollen up in her head, and sometimes in bed at night I imagined that my tongue was swollen too. My father said it was a terrible illness she had, just terrible, but I agreed with Holly: it was a terrible meanness. She was hellbent to make me as crazy as she was. Her speech was so halting it called to mind those patients shuffling down the dark hallway, the television light a beacon up ahead.

"Did Jack get seat belts. Installed."

"Frankly I'd just as soon hurl myself through the windshield."

"How can you. Say such a thing after. Holly."

But it wasn't even Holly that made her crazy, according to my father. She wasn't allowed to drive the car anymore, so she walked through town every day to the bluff by the bay, right out on River Street. Sometimes she braced herself on a big oak, staring at who knows what, at the bridge swinging open, at the islands out beyond our island. My father said it was better than staring at her bedroom walls but I wasn't so sure. Every girl in senior year took a turn asking if that wasn't my mother down on River Street, and they asked in a sweet pitying *God I'd kill myself if my mother was crazy* voice.

Jack Wesley moved on, to a cheerleader who was allowed to sit in his car without a seatbelt. Who could blame him? I was ready to move on myself, ready to go to college and never look back. When my mother asked me did I mean to major in French, I heard my voice go cruel and tight.

"No, I believe I'll learn some Russian or Chinese. Maybe some Vietnamese."

Look around you. Nobody takes French anymore. You stare at nothing all day but right here on the television there's a war going on and kids yelling through bullhorns. Maybe I won't even go to Carolina. Maybe I'll go somewhere they have a free speech movement. Maybe I'll go where they have a free LOVE movement. My mother said we were living in an age of infidelity and wickedness, and by God I was willing to be the first foot soldier in that new territory.

I'd never once been out on the river with a boy, the way every other girl in town had been. I couldn't even swim. Maybe Holly inherited our mother's disease and walked into the water with stones in her pockets. I started to wonder if I had it too, just a touch of it that kept me from being able to swallow sometimes.

* * *

My father moved out of the house and into the little apartment behind his agency, and you can be sure his eyes didn't meet mine when he told me his intention. My mother didn't even cry. "Why cry," she said, "when he's been lusting after his secretary all these long years, when he's been abandoning us all this while." The silence in our house echoed till I was sure I really had lost my mind, sure as she'd lost hers.

Now I was the one who had to stand over her morning and night to see she took her pills, and I was the one had to listen to her hymns. I should have seen the danger signs when her sentences came faster, when she took an interest in the linen closet again even though she didn't have a husband to keep house for anymore. Maybe I knew there wasn't a thing I could do to stop her.

This time when they called my name over the intercom I took my sweet time, but in the office my mother was nowhere to be seen. It was a phone call instead, and whose voice should I hear in the receiver but my father's secretary. She'd just seen my mother down at the boat ramp, wading in the water. Maybe somebody ought to go down there and see was she all right. She sure hoped the high school didn't mind, my getting a call like this.

They minded all right, they minded plenty, and so did I. I had to suffer the look the monitor gave me when I told her it was an emergency, and I had to walk past the boys blowing smoke rings in the parking lot, when what I wanted was to grab one of their cigarettes and run off in their cars and let my father's secretary take care of my mother. No. I turned over the engine and drove down the John C. Calhoun Road at the speed limit and turned the blinker when it was time to make a right.

By the time I parked in the corner of the parking lot, behind the stacks of Sunfishes and Sailfishes, I was steaming. And maybe more than that: maybe I was a little out of my mind myself. She was there at the bottom of the ramp, in broad daylight. She wore a big wide skirt, damp at the hemline. Was she wading out to drown herself, the way Holly did? I stood at the top of the ramp and called down:

"I want you to tell me right here and right now how did Holly drown in the river."

She swiveled round and gave me a quick-breaking grin, a little lopsided. I hadn't looked at her face in a long time, and in the bright daylight I saw how old she was, her powder caked in the lines running down her mouth. She still wore her lips cherry red when I'd been telling her nobody wore those bright shades anymore. When she opened her mouth I could see lipstick on her top teeth. She hadn't been taking those pills after all.

"Why what are you doing down here, sugar lamb?"

"Were you planning on drowning yourself too. You were. Weren't you."

She gave me a look that was begging me for something, the very same look that she gave that white-haired Episcopalian lady who was selling her Jesus pillow for a joke and didn't even understand my mother wanted to buy it for real. She was standing in water halfway to her knees.

"I said I want you to tell me were you going to drown yourself."

"You know better than that. I was just trying to get used to the water."

"So you could drown yourself."

"No, I don't think so."

She didn't THINK so? Maybe you can understand why at the moment I felt like pushing her into the water myself.

"How did Holly die."

Her upper lip crumpled. Why wasn't my father here, plucking her from the river. Why did he leave me to do it all alone.

"Is this where she drowned?"

"No, it wasn't here."

And I believed that much, because if you looked out from where we stood you couldn't see death or drowning at all. You saw the air and the water the same color as my mother's dyed hair, gold and silver mixed together. You saw an egret balancing itself on one stick leg out by the sandbar. You saw the old docks along the shore collapsing into the mud, the live oaks heaving down with moss, the tabby sea wall crumbling. You saw this town looking out on the bay so very pleased with itself, its big old white-columned houses fronting the water and its white teenagers sunning themselves in their sailboats, a town so smug it wouldn't even notice some middle-aged crazy lady wading out into the water in the middle of the day.

"She was sailing over yonder."

My mother never used a word like *yonder* with me: that was an upcountry word. She held her arm up, pointed out past the sandbar, out past the deep channel, out past the ends of the earth.

"She killed herself, didn't she."

"Where'd you get that idea, lambkin? You've had suicide on the BRAIN."

Well, who wouldn't have suicide on the brain, your mother saying you slept with your father, like you were in some Greek tragedy, and your father walking out like it was all your fault. I stared at her with no love in my heart whatsoever. Her hair was set into those tight old-fashioned curls she favored. She belonged on *Ozzie and Harriet*. She came from another time and another place, and furthermore she was crazy.

"Then tell me how did it happen."

This time she flinched, and crouched down in the water till her whole skirt was sopping wet. I put my hands on my hips and looked as stern as I knew how, and then she answered me as if we were having a normal conversation.

"She keeled over on that boy's boat."

"What?"

"She keeled over. They said it was her heart. It was . . . a freakish thing."

"But you always made it sound like she drowned."

"She died in a bikini."

"But you didn't even let her go out on the river."

"I couldn't stop Holly for beans! She never minded me the way you do."

I felt as if I'd had a heart attack myself, that I hadn't understood a single word put to me my entire life. Holly never drowned in the river? I was the good girl?

I waded in after her and her soaked skirt, thinking vicious thoughts. I wished she'd fight me off so I could twist her arms around her back. But she stood there docile, and she even reached her hand out for me to grab. I'd be damned if I'd take her hand. I circled round behind her and, when I pushed her up the ramp, she made a noise like a motorboat. I couldn't tell if she was crying over Holly or acting like a child again. I wanted to slap her silly.

But I led her to the car, and wrung out her skirt for her, and strapped her into her seatbelt. When I went around to the driver's seat she fixed a timid, obedient look on her face and commenced to humming a hymn, only she wasn't quite humming in alto range and she wasn't quite humming soprano. I revved the engine and she stopped humming altogether.

"I can't remember the words. Not so much as verse one."

Now she truly did sound like a child, puzzling out how you could lose words you'd known your whole life long. Well, I wasn't about to give her the verses to torment me with, but the look on her face was so confused that I heard myself say, "They'll come back."

She let out a big puttering sigh, and I knew I couldn't bear to take her home and listen to that sad sound. I drove over the bridge instead, so we could look down on the river where Holly did not drown, and sure enough she perked right up.

The afternoon light still shone gold and silver, and a red-sailed catamaran glided below us, looking for all the world like it was sailing into my mother's Age of Infidelity. The bay was just as unreal as a television screen. I wouldn't have been the least surprised to learn that my father and his secretary and Jack Wesley and even Dobie Gillis and his many loves were all sunning themselves down on that boat, while up here on the bridge I got to carry a carload of tormented Marines and old ladies hearing voices. I got to carry my mother, who chose the very moment we passed beneath the bridge tender's perch to burst out with the hymn she thought she'd forgotten:

"And are we yet alive! And see each other's face!"

She made it through all four verses, though she had to double back on some of them. I have never before or since heard a hymn sung at that reckless a pace. By the time I passed the shrimp docks she'd fallen into silence, and when I sneaked a peak I saw that she was sleeping like a baby.

OUR LAST STAND

— For Kevin Barry —

1.

IN THE NIGHT WE HEAR a moan, a woman's cry of pleasure or distress. Francie?

Groggy, we rise to peer out. *All well?* Gerard calls. *All well down there?*

A burst of riotous laughter. A gull's white form, a reverse silhouette in the night. Not Francie in peril, only one mad bird, a banshee shrieking over some cast-off it claims, a piece of bloody tissue or a bone or an eyeball. We've not seen a seagull in months. We thought them gone forever.

We squirm and twist through the stultifying night, cursing the sentimental day we imagined that coming here was a good idea, that staying on was wise.

2.

Cheery Gerard, up and about since the gull, greets me as I empty the slops. *Bit cooler today?*

The air presses down. The relentless sun's driven everyone out, everyone but the old, the infirm, those mad enough to fight like gulls over what remains. Everyone but the deluded.

It's not cooler, Gerry, you know it's not.

Behind us little-girl voices pipe a parody. *You know it's not.* We wheel to giggles from narrow faces: Francie's middle daughters, Maeve and Rachel, sprites from the next lane over. Their vests, light as moss, soak through with little-girl sweat. We've taken to wearing our skivvies, our jammies, the manky least we can possibly wear. All but Gerard, who wears white linen, stained with the dust of the drying city, ever so man-of-the-world. We chase Maeve and Rachel down the lane, Gerry roaring to their delight.

Gerry, don't say it's cooler.

Gerard, uncomplaining, smiles back, jowls drooping, tail fairly wagging. O Gerry, can't you see, despair shrouds the city. That gull stole our sleep, the heat is maddening, so very few are left behind.

Tom, my man, we'll see each other into old age yet.

We're old already, you wrinkled coot. I could turn a stout stick on Gerard and still not beat the good cheer from him.

3.

The scrum of boys arrives by nine, pounding our door, after our scant food. THRUMP THRUMP THRUMP. *Let us in, let us in.* Francie's eldest's in among them, wearing Gerry's cap, grubby hand on grubby nose—as if that will disguise him. Slow Eddie they call him.

Gerard bellows from upstairs the way Bernadette down the lane advises. *Out with yez, fecking morons.*

Once Gerry never let such a hurtful word cross his lips. Now look what pleasure he takes. He knows the lads will soon be back, hoping for a bit of chat to get them through the worst hours, claiming they had naught to do with the morning's extortion. Gerard will shake his fist, snatch back his cap, threaten to teach them baseball. Gerry will say they're only improvising till the world rights itself, as if the world could do such a thing.

4.

High noon. Lolling outside our window, Eddie hears his boyos call. He scampers off to the top of the lane but the gull blocks his way. We've been so long without them, the bird's a phantom to him now.

Talk to your man, Gerard advises. *Tell him your needs.*

Timid and small, Eddie advances, cap pulled low. *If you'll please lemme pass.*

When the gull bobs and weaves, mocking his sweet request, Gerard comes running, arms beating air. *Scat! Shoo!* The big bird, distracted, casts a cold eye. Slow Eddie slips past to his hooligan gang, hooting his joy.

5.

Now it's two gulls, brazen on the lane. Each tugs a broken mussel shell from the other's beak. They fight over ghost-flesh: all that's left is the memory of bivalve. The lunch hour.

Tommy: *When did we last see a gull so bold?*

Gerry: *When did we last see two?*

Old Bernadette, our counselor, hobbles down the lane in rose-colored peignoir. In her thin olive hair—a dye job gone bad—she's plaited strands of kelp. Drily she observes: *Looney-tunes.*

Gerry beams, as Gerry would. *Bird-brains,* he suggests. Without his cap, his bald pate gleams.

6.

The afternoon wears on. We keep a schedule, whose turn to collect the stools and chairs the other will whack for firewood. One forages in empty houses, the other cooks what little we find. One gathers kelp while the other makes camp on the powdery shore. Just now we linger, slumped against the day.

A sexual hum sounds through our dry old bones, a longing darker than any bloodlust that gang of hoodlums feels. Don't think we don't know what the other's after, framed so helpless against that door. Don't think the will to live is simply a thirsty tongue.

Gerard's the one to beat off aged lust. Dapper, sleeves rolled, he rallies and leaves me to tidy house, to hear floating whispers though no breeze blows.

Crossed an ocean to spend their last dime and still too daft to flee.

Our house is a stout stone bastion that once sheltered workers and vast swarms of children, then speculators, yuppies, insufferable hipsters. A fairy-tale house, two low-ceilinged stories, a dark lane north of the river. We fancied ourselves poets, intrepid ex-pats, countercultural geezers protesting the earth's demise. Where better than a rainy city?

Go back where yez came from, plummy faggots.

All our lives we dreamed of this country. Ours were the families who knew all the verses, we the lads partnering partnerless girls. We found each other early, two sentimental queers singing manly rebel songs. We tramped to this island for one last pilgrimage, wild joy in the roving of two old men. We'd die in this place—no use pretending, that was the plan. We'd nurse each other into the grave. We thought it a town where a neighbor might look in.

Go back or we'll send you back.

We didn't foresee the fevered city toasting brown. Folks like us headed for the mountains and took their money with them, but we're city folk and here we'll stay.

The river's emptied out, and with it the shops. The lights switched off, the wits and the wags heading for the hills. Let them wallow in mud. We lane-dwellers hear the dream-plunk of banjoes, the clink of glasses in the night. Our neighbor Ray moons us from his bedroom window, his one and only arm waving a martial beat. Sometimes, to get a rise, I say: *I'd like to get a pinch of that.*

Have at it, Gerry agrees, Ray's haunches white as moondust. *Make your move. Time's running out, don't delay.*

7.

Francie in her flowered nightie, buttercups on filmy green, knocks on our door.

I've come to ask yez a wee small favor.

We study her lithe frame, her wiry black curls. Four fathers for her six, and the latest, Albert M, took an interest in the brood. He's after water now, gone six weeks and more. She reads our thoughts and frets: *Where can Albert be?*

On the lane, we've written him off, gone down our list for an able-bodied man to commandeer a cart. We're urban cowboys, tumbleweeds rolling through our frazzled brains. Francie's dreaming too, a fist to her breast.

Now Francie, you're not thinking of taking off after him? Our old hearts clatter.

I am, she says, *and none too soon. The gulls are the sign, wouldn't they be?*

But you'll have to cross the Midlands!

They say in the Midlands we'll drink from cow teats. Will we tell her that surely the cows lie dead in the field? Does she think the baby will walk to the Midlands?

We hover instead, gallant hosts. *You'll have a cup of tea?* What we mean's a spoon of water wasted on nettles.

She smiles a gentle no. *Will yez walk us to the quay? I want to see my little monsters make a marching line. And if they can, tomorrow then . . .*

Our hearts cave in.

8.

And so she parades all six of her ducklings, each one pinching the child who's littler still. Off we all tramp, down to the quay. We rarely turn this way these days: to gather the kelp, we head to the shore. Now, on our march, we compose a long dirge. We mourn the loss of Maeve and Rachel. We mourn Slow Eddie, resourceful and sly. Francie will go, we know she will, and won't we be tempted to follow her lead? Her choice is our choice: west or east, country or town, drown or parch. We've heard the storms are fierce avengers. Above, the sky is striped with gulls.

You're frightened of floods, sweet Francie girl?

Of course I am, she answers wisely. *And birds give us all a proper fright.*

We halt at the bridge. Below, where the murky river ran, lies a bed of black like hard dry shit, the city's organs parched. The air smells of dung and crushed oil.

Shrill light. Behind the quay, brick walls crumble. The children swat at a trio of gulls. Is a city to children what it is to old men? Are their neighbors a posse protecting their dreams? The lunatic shrieks are a lonesome sound.

We stare each other down, Cheerful Gerry and Hard Tommy, each thinking the other's thought. Who will look in on us now?

Francie scans the sky, Maeve and Rachel whimper, the baby babbles on. The trio of gulls drops its orbit lower still. Francie swipes her neck. She hoists the baby to her hip, her own boldness vanished.

The menacing gulls flap at our heads. Slow Eddie squats, clutching Gerry's cap. Francie cries: *The gulls on the road—oh, what will I do.*

Home! Gerry cries, and homeward we flee.

9.

Evening glaring, we hold our council right in the lane. The gulls swarm to block our path, mocking us with their flaps and feints, delighting when we flinch. Ray hauls himself out, shorts hitched high, to spit at the birds and taunt them too: *Pluck out our eyes. Go on, go on.*

The children, we warn, but not in time: Eddie wails and the rest chime in. Gerry whispers, *Hush, chickadees. The birds only tell us the rain's on its way.*

We all close our eyes and pretend to hear thunder. *No, Gerry, no. Don't say it one more time.*

Don't say it, echoes Maeve.

Won't you come with us after Albert M? Francie looks to us, two knobby old men, while the gulls screech disdain. Ray sneers, too, as if to say, *Them! They didn't make it past the quay.*

The birds press closer still. We can't read the gulls. We can't read each other in the dimming light. I search Gerry's eyes and find the same mad hope I see each dawn.

Nothing good's decided by dark, he proclaims. *By morning, we'll know what to do.*

Tonight Sweet Francie will stay in our house, our thin soup her children's soup. We all agree: another night. We'll take our stand together. In the morning, we'll count the gathering gulls, and then we might go. If Francie leaves, we might leave too.

10.

A screech of gulls takes up watch at the top of the lane. We measure how deep the water pours. The children play with the blade that scrapes shriveled carrot, sweet carrot smell filling our throats. We sip our slimy kelp. Three spoons for each and then to bed, remembering scallops, the butter poured thick.

I'll moon you, fecking morons, Ray calls across the lane.

11.

We crowd each other, shifting dry bones in the feather bed. Woolly heat surrounds us. The thirst is fearsome. *Jesus,* the children rasp in their sleep. *Please forgive us.*

Eels slither round our legs. I wake to Gerry's toes climbing my calves. Panic puffs its rank air hot in my face. We'll die without water. We're dying now. First dawn, we'll beg whisky from Ray, drink for the children so their ends will be quick. We'll clutch each other, dying, singing bloody rebel songs.

I wake to murmurs—*Gerry, sweet Gerry*—but I've only wakened myself. I feel a fool. The thick crust of his nails presses onto the soles of my feet, a sign I cannot fathom in my fear. Forgive me, Gerry, please. I don't believe we'll make it through to morning. I don't believe we can.

12.

But we wake, we do, to the first blush of light. The clatter of wheels: I strain to hear, but Gerry's up, a flash of white. *It's Albert M, surely it is.*

You're raving, man.

Francie rises with him, the pair of them on fire. They fly down the stairs, into the black. I stand at the window to watch Gerry's nightshirt shining in moonlight, his bony feet bare against the brick lane. In the corner of the sill, a spindly dove hides from the gulls.

Gerry's hope has gone too far. Look how he brushes past the diving gulls. Look how they race to greet their hero. Look how fearless Francie is, skipping toward a ghost.

13.

Can it be we're all dreaming, hearing hooves clop? Do we all chase a ghost? We tumble downstairs as brown light gathers, the baby I carry a handful of dust.

If it's a vision, we see it together. Gerry leads the wagon, the pony solemn, a faithful acolyte. Atop the cart, Francie and her man sit high, Francie a dollop of cream in her green nightie, Albert gaunt and worldly, porkpie hat pushed back just so. Francie twists to show us his haul: barrels of water, baskets of roots, a few days of life. We're all too shy to meet his eye.

Bernadette hobbles down the lane, presses peignoir flat with swollen hands. *Albert M! You're welcome home. News from the West?*

No news that's good news, he calls to greet her. *I have your water here.* Our chieftain now, he jumps from his cart and never so much as skews his crown. Francie hops down too to urge him on. He draws a massive breath from his cavernous belly. *No news that's good news,* didn't he say? A hush falls over us, his words a shadow on the fast-rising sun.

Finally he begins: *The floods are cascading all through the West.* We conjure the scene in the pause he gives us. Mud roars down the rocky slopes, the ocean lashes the stony shore.

Fighting's broken out. Many are maimed. We hear Albert's voice catch on a nail and know to wait patient for more. Albert M's a man of few words. Perhaps this is all he has for us now. But no, he fills his lungs and starts anew. We brace each other as he tells the news:

Pikes, axes, butcher knives. Anything to hand. Even the gulls sidle closer together. Poor Eddie, stroking the pony's mane, shakes hard enough to set the beast aquiver. And Albert, seeing the children suffer, stills his tongue, but presently fills the void:

More refugees than you can picture. We picture them so, a wagon train from coast to coast, men on foot stumbling alongside. We picture our Albert, the barrels careening, the great long night swallowing him up.

I've dropped a load of them south of the river, says Albert M, and we all do our best to take in his meaning. The city's come home? Already they forage the houses we forage. Already, then, they prowl the shore.

Tomorrow, he says, *I'll go fetch more.*

Francie's head hangs in shocked sorrow but, queenly, she says: *Of course. You must.*

The last lights off the black West went, says Francie's man.

All our heads bob and bow. The priests have gone into hiding here, but poets are always out and about. Francie signs the cross, Ray spits at the gulls, Gerry sniffs the air for weather portents and signs of more life still.

I'll need to take Bernie for her good counsel. Ed, you'll come for muscle, lad.

This news hits Francie hard. Her golden head drops lower still and then she unspools a keen, her sorrow hard and true. Across the pony's mane, her hand reaches for her son's. He squeezes back, flush with a joy he can't suppress: Albert needs him. Bernie joins in wailing to make a chorus, but soon enough they wind the crying back. The city's come home: there's so much to see to.

The rest of us stand stunned and still. Three of our number, off to the West, off to the war that wages there.

14.

We came to die where a neighbor might look in.

The gulls gather and rise from the lane. Bright wings fill white sky. Look at our Eddie, grooming that pony. Look at our Francie, smooching with her man in the hours they have left. The dawn has broken full, the light a sheet of foil shining, but in the distance great clouds roll. Surely that's a rumble we hear.

Have the barrels at the ready, Bernie bellows. *Pots and pans and rubbish bins.*

And Gerry adds, as Gerry would: *The rain should flush the scallops.*

Bit cooler? Ray suggests. *A little bit cooler, I'd wager, today.*

SHOULD I BE AFRAID?

H<small>E'S BEEN LISTENING FOR THE WHIRR</small> of the woods, but what he hears sounds human: a dream voice, female. When he lifts the shutter slat, there she is in the bright early-morning haze. She won't see him inside the dark hut, staring out—wait, not *staring*. Glancing. If they question him, he'll say: *Heard a noise, glanced outside.* He'll totally deny staring at her—whoa. Think the word, you'll slip. Maybe not today, maybe not tomorrow, but eventually that syllable will follow the circuit right down, brain to tongue, so do not whatever you do think it. *Body part* is safe, if he needs to deny. *I was definitely not staring at her body part.* He says it three times in his head. As recommended.

She's kneeling, bent over, body part raised in the air. Through the chinks he hears her whisper sweet somethings to a marsh lily that's migrated up here. Nell used to talk to the plants too: *Come on, little buddy, moving you out of the sun, this won't hurt a bit.* He lifts the slat again. This time, she maybe senses him: she's kind of swaying that body part. He could go out to the sani-hut, take a piss—not *piss*, even *whiz* is no good. Anyway, what kind of introduction is a trip to the sani?

First thing he has to do is stop twitching. Has to breathe, take it in. If he can hold his tongue, the hut's all his for the next three years. The palmetto bark's thin as walls get, but it's all he needs in this heat, more than he hoped for. One table, one chair, one light-fixture on auto-time. The cot's covered with mosquito netting—might as well be silk sheets. Once he's sure the ProtectAll has a good view of the floor planks, he'll pull that mattress down off the sagging springs. Keep his hands on his chest, make sure they don't think he's giving any body parts a tug.

Second thing he has to do: the before-sleep chores Orientation Guy demonstrated twice. A pipe descends from the ceiling to fill two laundry buckets, wash and rinse. He peels off his dirty shirt for the first bucket. "Greetings, Protect-All, I'm washing my shirt now, sudsa." He hums, feels like an idiot, rinses twice as instructed. "Don't worry, little buddy, this won't hurt a bit." He gives the shirt a good squeeze and then another. "Here I go, ProtectAll, out to the line"—where, just coincidentally, she still kneels nearby.

She's wearing the leisure. The work uniforms are drab green (*two is-sued—wash one each reverse-day*), the leisure drab brown. Detains and work-releasers don't get sun gear: you used to see melanomas popping before your very eyes, but since the fog who even needs sun gear? On her the military cut of those shorts looks—Stop. Right. There. *The most offensive language slips are the ones we make only to ourselves.*

She flattens her palm to the ground. "Don't worry, he won't hurt you."

She's telling the marsh lily not to worry? They've made her shit-ass bonkers. Oh jeez oh jeez. Control the language. Anyway, a minute ago he was telling the shirt in the bucket not to worry. They're all bonkers now.

She's up, all her body parts, offering her hand: "It's OK, it's allowed."

Bare-chested, he shakes the male-to-female. She has a long sun-hardened arm, skinny legs. Her hair's a halo of rusty dark frizz. "Don't move an inch. The mics don't pick up here."

"The PAs still see us talking."

"I'm allowed to orient—" she points to the facility—"a new worker."

"OK, thanks. I'm, uh, Ricky Lee Flint."

"Oh. Maybe call yourself Rick while you're here?"

"Yeah, all right." She probably sees his grimace—the ProtectAll definitely sees. A marble drops down his gullet.

She plays casual again: "What they get you for?"

"I was charged with lip. Plus ambivalence."

At that she lets out a sweet little hoot. "Better not say it like that."

"Better roll over and die?"

"There's the lip."

"Glad you still recognize it." What's the matter with him, two days out? She could get him slapped right back in. He tries again but can't help the sneer: "I'm enthusiastically male."

"Well, I'm Fantelle Lacey. I'm your work partner and I'm enthusiastically female."

Either she just mimicked his sneer or they're soulmates. Seriously? She was in for ambivalence too? "They give you that name, Fantelle?"

"Watch it. Sleep alarm, any second."

He does watch it: in the brightening reverse-day, he watches her fantelle retreat. They want him enthusiastically male? His body parts do their bit, but knowing the PA's watching his hard-on—think *inflation,* say *inflation*—deflates him fast. On that crazy day when every micro-mic in their dorm was shut down for ten blessed minutes, the detens indulged in an orgy of speculation about the Protect-Alls: were they manned? Womanned? Botsied? Or did they just keep a tally of every time you moved, shat, dreamt the wrong way?

The whole line of thinking's so far beyond verbot. Get a grip.

* * *

He's on the reverse-night shift. Sleepless in the light, he ate the breakfast ration hours ago: cold protein lumps, seven hard raisins, powdered milk to mix with cistern-water. He forced down the whole bowl, stinking of sulfur, but he's still starving. So what else is new?

His turn showering's not till Night Four, so he fetches his shirt off the line in the damp and dreamy dusk. Miracle he ever made it out to work-release. He hears water running in the sani-hut, tries not to go visual, doesn't even smell his own funk till he's back inside, pulling on his damp shirt, listening for the rap at the door.

He's replayed his conversation with Fantelle all the sleepless day, but seeing her come to fetch him at dusk qualifies as a vision: she's a silhouette framed by the doorway, her hair wild in the mist. Dream-woman? Test? She leads him around the cluster of huts where, he learned yesterday, the entire staff for their little unit lives. The four of them work twelve-hour shifts, seven days a week, but it's low infection risk, easy work. Also ironic work, since he's just spent three years under the supervision of b-guards. Now he'll learn to be a botsie-wrangler.

Fantelle fairly trots on the dirt path sloping down to their marshside unit and he speedwalks alongside her, new muck boots pinching, bugs nursing at his shins.

"Overcrowded," she's saying. "Up to one-oh-three if everybody made it through the night."

"Any of them ever get so depressed—"

She shakes her head, a warning. "Randomized listening through here."

They pass through disfigured pine and underbrush on both sides: the dusk is falling fast now but he can't help tracing the trees' jagged outlines. The taller pines, the healthier ones, call to mind b-guards lined up in full gear.

Micro-mics and PAs could be anywhere, everywhere. A blister simmers: right big toe. Above, the first sign of stars, unless he's hallucinating, which isn't out of the question. Every other tree-trunk on the border is tagged with a little square solar night-light. The transport guy said the facility was seventy-five miles from deep deten—down here, they get as much as a week of sun, which is why they gave him the reverse-night shift, so he won't go into light-shock.

Weird to be out, to see the kind of woods he tramped through as a kid. At the deten camp he didn't see much: the superfog swirled and settled like the gray gravy that disguised their indistinguishable mounds of so-called food. Visibility was so low management had to reverse reverse-day—unlike the rest of the overheated country, the detens went back to working days, sleeping nights. Even in daylight, though, the b-guards didn't dare let them cross the yard, much less work off the gray gravy. They marched through hot dense fog tied like kindergarteners to a rope. On their way to re-ed, one building over, the botsies made them chant: *Hi-ho, hi-ho.* He hears Hardy chanting, mocking, a half-beat behind him. Do not vocalize, do not verbalize, do not go there.

The facility comes into view, a string of connected pole barns laid end to end like a braked train painted acid-green to shine through fog. His unit—theirs—is on the end: Far East. Orientation Guy said the barns were light enough to pull apart and ship to higher ground if a superstorm passed through. Flint asked what happened to the residents then but the guy said: *We don't cover that in Orientation.*

Now he stands on the threshold of Far East, trying to remember if he should hold the door for Fantelle or if that's verbot. He's fit to piss his pants. Wee his pants. Christ, he's antsy. That perfume of mud and rot and swamp gas you get in the lowcountry wafts. Fantelle holds the door herself.

Don't lose hope, buddy, this won't hurt a bit.

Inside, the lights are dimmed, most of the residents sleeping—it's only seven o'clock—but the joint's jumping. Botsies boogie up and down two rows of beds: looks like the field hospital in an old war holo. Fantelle doesn't trouble to whisper, just explains in a normal training voice that they're busy with wake-up meds: *jollies*. The botsies look jolly too. They don't trigger the level of guard-panic he's braced for.

Today, all he's supposed to do is shadow Fantelle. He tries not to conclude definitively that she's a test, because then he'll have to figure out how to pass, how to demonstrate enthusiastic attraction while simultaneously demonstrating total control. It's not just her body parts: he's turned on by her talking to the marsh lily, knowing where the mics were. Do. Not. Go. There. Anyway she thought *Ricky Lee,* which happens to be his real name, sounded too ambi, plus she walks so damn fast he's mainly trying to keep up. Another blister, other foot. She brings him to the bald management guy who's here to wrangle while he shadows.

The shake goes OK: Flint's worked a lot on the male-to-male. "Bob," Management Guy says. First names? That's a test.

"Rick." When Bob waddles off without comment, he's ambivalently grateful for Fantelle's name advice. She's already heading in the opposite direction, wearing a small victory smile. She stops at a bed where a botsie spoons med-filled supersauce into a geezie's maw. In the low lights Flint sees a living cadaver, male or female he couldn't say. Must be a hundred and ten. A little cap of sparse white hair, pink skull underneath covered with scabs that look like glyphs. Mouth open, jaw locked. The botsie spoons in sauce, closes the jaw. "Swallow." The geezie flinches and swallows without opening its crusted eyes.

Fantelle says: "Alisdair baby, what's new?" *Baby?* Flint, rising to the balls of his feet, goes all fight-flight.

She feels his panic. "We're allowed three endearments for the botsies: *baby, sweetheart, honey.* Old offensive words for useful new purposes, to help us job-bond." She twists her body, probably so her face is out of PA-view: "Now I'd like you to repeat what I just said, because you'll have to train shadows too." She's raised one perfectly arched eyebrow.

He forgives her for finding *Ricky Lee* ambi. He might forgive her anything. He wants to reach out and stroke her cheek; even in these dim lights he can trace the sun's work, the start of crow's feet and neck rings. She's got to be at least ten years older, the recommended female/male gap. His sisters were older, too: Patsy by four years, Nellie two. This is no accident, his assignment to shadow Fantelle, his hut next door. He leaps forward to a sanctioned-mate future: management decides that Fantelle's genes will revive his reprobate DNA. She becomes the poster-ambi-gone-good, promoted to supplies, where she occasionally lifts a bottle of meds. The two of them live on the edge, getting high on purloined pills, putting out feelers for the resistance. At night. . . Focus. Focus. She's saying: "Repeat after me," and because he's aces at repeating he says it perfectly three times, as recommended.

When he's on the last rep, he takes a good look at Alisdair: tin-can model. Old folks can't handle the uncannys or the hyperreals. Alisdair's cartoon face is like the first Preacher prototypes: painted eyes, smattering of lashes, nose a less-than caret. His gestures are scary-smooth but Alisdair, permanently half-smiling, doesn't exactly scare him. Fantelle tells him for the second time that the wranglers are only there to correct and adjust. No talking to the residents: that's the botsie's job. Chatting would only confuse them. She skips ahead to the next botsie.

"Neville sweetheart, how's it going?"

"Going crazy." Neville's programmed for cheeseball, and Flint's not sure he can handle cheeseball just yet. In deten, cheeseball botsies stuck men's heads in clogged toilets for saying *piss* or *shit* and then made cheeseball jokes: *Potty mouth,* they'd chortle, pressing the head down.

Two beds over, Alisdair's moved on to wrestle a howling pink-hair fighting the stretchy HumaneStrap. The botsie hoists her up, plops her at her motowalker, and escorts her down the first rec area, where she can wobble out her anxiety. Flint channels the muscle-memory of being wrestled by a b-guard and feels his own bruises blooming. But here nobody goes to the hole, here between every twenty beds are areas where residents, like toddlers, are redirected. Yesterday at Orientation they let him sit at the first redirect, an old-timey listening station with surround-phones. So long since he heard canned music his mind went blank, but finally he chose "Can I Get a Witness," his mother's favorite oldie. Talk about cheeseball. He had to stop after a few bars of Marvin Gaye's aching voice—they're not going to see one spark of emotion out of him. The second area's a holo station, where geezies can hold hands with their favorite stars. He declined to sample that experience, hoping instead for the massage box down in the third redirect. Orientation Guy never offered the massage.

Neville—also tin-can, more of a butler get-up—glides over to an old lady crying out: "Are those children naked?"

Neville answers in a debonair British accent. "No, madam, they have nice new suits."

"I wanted to teach them a lesson," she insists. "That's why I quit drinking."

"That was a sound decision."

"Should I be afraid?"

"Madam," Neville says, "there is nothing whatsoever to fear."

She pulls her mouth taut. "Are those children naked?"

The entire exchange goes on auto-repeat, like the rest of his first three hours. He tries to imagine that old lady with naked children as his grandmother, but he never met a grandmother, so he pictures his sisters instead.

Fantelle says: "Break time. Go sit for five in any redirect."

He hobbles to the empty holo station and stares out through the big window cut into the steel. It's deep reverse-night now, so he has to imagine the marshside view: the live oaks that have survived, still majestic, still draped in dangling moss that covers them like hair shirts. Below the bluff, a little carpet of pluff mud leads to the marsh with its tangles of watery life. The cypresses stand beyond, serene.

Swamp Fox territory. Wouldn't Mr. Millen get a kick out of that? In Constitutional Heroes class, Mr. M called Francis Marion a *guerilla freedom-fighter.* Mr. M thought the whole Constitutional-Guard regime was bogus, anti-constitution if you read the actual document, but of course he never said that out loud. Instead, he quizzed his students on how far the Swamp Fox would go: *Would he shoot a man in the back? Would he turn tail and run?* They all knew Mr. M was about to run himself the day he asked: *Would the Swamp Fox let himself be chipped?*

Mr. M only made it two weeks in the woods before the grab—but Flint's always believed that those two weeks kicked off the movement. Not that the movement got what it wanted: the only ones to get the exemption were certified whites on the Southern coast, the CG's base. Flint's not exactly their base, and he's not exactly certified, but the CGs decided if he was white enough for school he was white enough for the exemption. His father's missing, his mother's a lifer, but he's escaped the chip. So far.

* * *

One day's training, that's it. Next day, Fantelle works her way up one line of beds while Flint works his way down, already bored out of his language-free mind. The two of them circle up, down, and back, blisters blazing, overseeing botsies who need no oversight, who keep up a steady cluck of soothing conversation. It's nothing like deten, where he was always wide-awake, always playing defense against the b-guards and his fellow detains: raging, sex-starved inepts. . . not *sex-starved.* Conjoinment-starved.

At midnight, a distraction arrives. A middle-aged, creative type—long forelock, jumping sandals—wheels his mother, an incoming, into her placement. The new geezie's out of it, slumped in her motochair. Creative Type says: "So cheerful, Mom! You're going to love autonocare." On his way out, bouncing along, he leers at Fantelle.

A few hours later, another distraction: Fantelle's botsie, Sadie, scoots away to stop a gent strangling himself with the HumaneStrap. Fantelle's old lady watches the rescue with a gaze as unsettling as a hawk's, and Fantelle sidles closer to her. A fine dark moustache perches above the old lady's lip. She sits up on her own, a striped shawl on her shoulders, fringes dangling. She has to have an exemption for those fringes.

In the midst of the commotion with the suicidal geezie, Fantelle murmurs something to her. Flint lip-reads the next words loud and clear—"Poor old dude." Talking to the geezies is definitely verbot, so Fantelle must know she's beyond range the way she did outside. He's impressed: willing to take the risk under Bob's nose—she must have done serious time in deten, where learning the grids, calculating the tiny zones where the micro-mics don't pick up, is serious mind-labor, and passing on the knowledge is sacred ritual.

He braces, waiting for Neville and Alisdair and Sadie to swivel their heads, the botsie threat display. But they don't crank, meaning they didn't get a signal, meaning Fantelle's calculated the mic-free zone perfectly and kept herself out of PA view besides. And now she's passed on that knowledge to him. He studies Shawl Lady as she studies him: looks like one of his teachers, fixing to zap him. His balls—not *balls, repro-tanks*—twinge. *Repro, repro.* How much of that did Shawl Lady follow? How much does she know?

When Fantelle leaves her to go to Sadie's side, the old woman does her best to beckon him with a rigid finger. Flint sends her a sad smile that's supposed to say *Sorry, ma'am,* then pivots fast because he might have already triggered some algorithm that counts how long you were looking.

* * *

On the walk home, Fantelle waits till they're midway to whisper: "She's a rabbi." The trees look prehistoric in the breaking dawn. The air's fit to bust with humidity and now this info, the weight of it pressing on all sides. He should have trusted Fantelle from Day One. He shouldn't trust her even now. He's never seen a rabbi much less a lady rabbi—only Christers allowed in deten—but *prayer shawl* emerges from deep memory.

A rabbi. But what if the micro-mics just randomly picked up Fantelle's voice? What if they're listening in this very minute?

"There it is. The rabbit." His voice, spontaneous and wildly enthusiastic, takes him by surprise. He points out an imaginary creature for the PAs.

Fantelle plays right along. "Foxes in these woods, too."

A smile overtakes him, the first smile in forever. "Swamp foxes." He starts to laugh and before he knows it, he's laughing hard enough to choke. He dizzies with the stupidity of letting himself go. What's the punishment for hysteria? What's the punishment for saying *swamp fox*?

Fantelle, quiet as death, sets her face blank as a sheet of fog.

* * *

He braces himself for the punishment, but no one comes for him that day or the next. Management waits weeks, waits for the day Sadie's rough, wiping the rabbi's mouth. One thing Flint's learned about the rabbi: she won't take disrespect from the bots. This day, shawl askew, she pushes the botsie's hand away with her forearm and cries out in some ancient language. Fantelle rushes toward her.

Every botsie in their unit cranks. A mesmeric whirring begins: he didn't even know they could produce a sound like that, a chorus like insects or snakes. Fantelle wraps her long arms around the rabbi. It's so beyond ver-bot, what Fantelle's doing right now, that there's got to be another word. *Verbotener?*

He watches Fantelle with such horror that it takes him too long to reg-ister Neville behind him, making the grab, using the two-elbow wrench. He thinks his shoulders might come out of their sockets and hears himself groan. The rabbi abandons her ancient language to holler: "This is an outrage!"

Flint calls: "It's all right, I'm all right," which just tripled, maybe qua-drupled, his punishment. Meanwhile Alisdair's peeled Fantelle away from the rabbi and grasps her elbows while Sadie, smug and relentless, carries on wip-ing the rabbi's mouth.

Bob—hey, he hasn't seen Bob in a while—strides down the middle aisle, bald pate shimmering. Flint fights the urge to repeat his hysterical laughter. With each and every grab, he's acted like a little kid who just doesn't get what's going down.

"Take them to their quarters," Bob barks and flourishes his meaty hand, calling for botsie back-ups.

* * *

So. Your hut's your own private hole. He doesn't need a thermostat to feel it pass one hundred in mid-morning. Humidity builds all through reverse-day, when nobody could possibly sleep, when he can only prickle, sting, swat. Haze glares through the hut's slats and chinks till the torrents commence mid-afternoon: the rain comes in waves, the lightning taunting him. He hears limbs crack, hesitate, thud. He rises to lift the slat—with so much of the coast washed away, the instinct's perverse, but he's always loved the storms. The b-guards crank from every direction. OK, so he's not allowed to look out.

No light or food, either, but they haven't shut off the cistern-water yet. Like a dog, he laps from his bowl, lowers himself to the mattress again. He feels the zaps to come in every coiled muscle. His balls, his *repro-tanks*, recede deep into his body. He sleeps in snatches and wakes as if he's a geezer himself, too stiff to straighten. The stench of his own piss and shit—*wee* and *do*, he can still do it—is a torment: no botsie enters to empty the bucket. They'll let him play it out in his head till his fear builds like the moisture, till the pressure makes him blow. Then he won't care anymore. He'll say anything, but anything won't be good enough. They'll zap and zap until they get bored, till they don't care either.

The storms seep into the hut. He pulls himself up from the sagging mattress to let muddy water sluice over his blisters, carbuncles by now. Whatever gunk's in that rain will make the infection worse, but a spiking fever would get him to another level, a higher plane. The water rolls down the planks' incline: there goes salvation.

* * *

Day four of solitary. Or five. Those fuckers—those management dudes, those Bobs—made him lose track. He pictures what Fantelle's enduring next door. If she's enduring anything. The b-guards act out the whole sham, so you never know who ratted you out, the PA or the micro-mic or the human being you briefly trusted. He drifts and floats on a scummy soup. Fantelle strokes herself, taunting him like the lightning. He doesn't recognize himself: he's cruel as a Constitutional Guard, standing over her with a riding crop to lash the ambivalence out of her. He's never conjoined with a woman—he's never conjoined with anyone. He was sixteen when they grabbed him, a shy kid who'd been on mandatory home-schooling till he was ten, till Patsy was old enough to take over the household. After they carted his mother away, Patsy enrolled him in secondary, but when they nabbed him he wasn't even close to making any moves or even knowing who to make them to. He only knew that he was OK with all that was humanly possible and miserably innocent of every possibility. In deten, big men with no teeth leered at the new ambi, but the b-guards would have torn the toothless men's balls off on the spot if they so much as sounded a smooch: plenty of detains swore they'd personally witnessed the bloody deed. B-guards, their armor reinforced, moved fast. They could break up a fight, or a rape, before you'd seen it start. The ProtectAll always saw it first.

During the detens' one brief interlude of micro-mic freedom, though, that strange and wondrous day, hard Hardy briefly rockabillied his pelvis against him. Hardy was a motherboard genius with big plans to liberate them all, but the botsies were poised, line after line of them, latched onto triggers. Maybe the mics were off but when Hardy realized the PAs were still on, he backed away slowly as a stripper in an old holo, with a rueful smile. *Some other time.* Then the b-guards came to drag him away.

Hardy always wore the same contemptuous look Patsy gave him, mean as a coon ready to bite his hand off but still full of some weird sympathy: for Flint's stupidity, his innocence. Hardy's in the room with him now, pressing up against him. Flint jerks his hand off his crotch. Hardy. Fantelle. The damp press of human flesh. Stop. Stop it.

He's weak past hunger. He'll be a bag of pine needles when they drag him off, but he'll fight. He'll flight. He'll be the Swamp Fox, feather in his cap, swinging from a rope of braided Spanish moss tied with a possum tail. He shimmies up a live oak, burrows into its deep crook, its sweet mushy-pussy. A prehistoric clump-clump sounds: a sea turtle, come to lay her eggs.

It's the rabbi, wiping his forehead the way his mother used to do. "Rabbi," he begs. "How can I be a man?"

The rabbi's touch is silken. "Do you want to be a man?"

"I want to be a swamp fox."

"They'll throw sand in your eyes." The rabbi presses her fingers down on his brow. "They'll garble the words."

He feels his panic rise. "The words don't work anymore."

She presses harder. "Use the old words."

"I'll tear them to shreds."

She rolls her eyes. "Blessed are you, Lord God, who has not made me a man."

"What do I do?"

"Put down that riding crop."

Her hand falls away and he looks up: a hawk circles his hut, sweet Nellie in its beak. The hawk is furious but Nell's serene, indifferent. He's the one crying out, rubbing his sand-filled eyes. He opens them gingerly.

There seems to be a botsie in his hut: it's good old Preacher Alisdair. Flint didn't hear the door creak. He didn't finish the vision. He doesn't want Alisdair, he wants the rabbi back, the rabbi and his sisters. He kind of even thought he might get a glimpse of his mother, though if he lets himself picture his mother, he'll lose his mind.

Alisdair plays it cruel, humming "Can I Get a Witness" as he plops a tin of grub on the table. "Eat up." Wasn't his accent suave before? Now it's snarly. If this is real. If Flint's really awake. The botsie's mocking voice reaches him underwater, but the smell of stewed greens, rich as swamp gas, pulls him to the surface.

"Back to work," Alisdair says. "Chop-chop." Hoisting the honey bucket, the botsie *tsks-tsks* clicks of contempt. Flint watches him heave the bucket through the door, sees mounds of indistinguishable food on the table, manages to hoist his whooshing head upright.

Chop-chop.

* * *

It's a new game entirely. Sadie arrives to escort them back to work, but at the unit Bob's nowhere to be seen. No zapping: the botsies don't even threaten it. He and Fantelle go about their duties. The bags under Fantelle's eyes age her another decade. She won't look his way.

Somehow he makes it through the night without passing out. The next dusk, he finds three extra raisins and a double-portion of powered milk in his rations. This is mind-fucking like he's never experienced. *Mind-messing, mind-messing.* No. Mind-fucking: he wills the full sound to form, replays it. An old word.

Sadie escorts them back and forth now: that's the only difference. The snatches of conversation he can't have with Fantelle are holes in his head. When the lady who didn't know if she should be afraid dies in her sleep, he finds himself scanning the night sky. There's less of it to see as the fog finally rolls in, its thickening gradual, familiar. Inside the unit the rabbi twists herself, dawn and dusk, to take its measure as it settles on the marsh.

Weeks of impenetrable fog. On the first day sun breaks through, a voice—Bob's?—comes over the surround-speakers. "We regret to announce a superstorm approaching." The voice is offhand, lulling. "Please take your stations."

Fantelle approaches to tell him they're cleared to speak to each other for the duration of the evacuation. Her voice is back to normal volume, with a new little tremolo. "I've got the botsies sorting meds. You take the worker-b's. They have to wheel the geezies down to West."

West? Fantelle hears his thoughts again: "A skeleton crew stays—worker-b's and b-guards."

Skeleton crew sounds as ominous as *West*. In the superstorm that flooded deten, he was neck-deep for a night and a day, with only a skeleton crew to guard them. The water would have covered his mouth and nose, but the other detens showed him how to stand on a rolled-up pallet. In the beginning, the Christers hollered out, "Jesus, Jesus!" but after twelve hours of balancing on a sodden pallet and treading water, one of the short guys screamed, "Screw Jesus!" A b-guard on telescopic legs stretched into the muck and throttled him on the spot, probably for the *screw* and not for the *Jesus*.

The geezer-transfer's slow going. Bed by bed, worker-b's wheel the geezies down the center aisle of each unit till they reach the last one, Far West, where they squeeze the beds in, six inches apart. The old folks are double-dosed with calmies, but the meds take a while to kick in and meanwhile their whimpers leave Flint drenched: when a frightened geezie cries, his upper body leans in that direction till sense pulls it back the other way. He's beginning to understand why Fantelle couldn't stop herself from hugging the rabbi.

When Far West is full, they start filling Near West, the other unit that will stay on the ground. Those CG managers are cold, cruel men. He repeats it as a mantra—*Those managers are cold, cruel men*—till it's time to transfer their own unit. He picks up mantra-speed when they move the rabbi. The other geezies lie flat, oblivious, but she's wide awake, reciting what can only be prayers. They park her in the dead middle of a middle row. Does he risk a good-bye? Backing away, he raises his hand at his waist but the rabbi, head lowered, doesn't see. She's peaceful, he wants to say, but that's only the lie Patsy told them about their mother's removal: *Didn't you see how peaceful she looked?*

At dawn, Bob directs them to sleep for an hour in Far East, Fantelle in the dead geezie's bed. Flint takes the floor, shaking with fatigue, but somehow manages to drift off. He wakes in the eerie emptiness of their unit, the rabbi's absence almost a presence. The light outside is clear and golden, the way it always gets before the supers. The big box-transports idle outside.

They're ready for full dismantle when management turns the power off one unit at a time, West to East. That means the micro-mics and PAs are out, too, but Flint feels more naked than ever. Outside, the sky's cobalt. Small animals—bony squirrels, malformed possums—still limp along for higher ground. That means they have some time. He listens to a lumbering thump: a trio of gators passing the big marshview window. He urges Neville along——"Pick it up, pick it up"—as they make their way through the dim buildings for final check. God, he's starting to sound like Bob.

In Near West, Bob does a last run-through with Alisdair and Sadie, Flint's old tormentors. If they know how to mock him, do they know how to be afraid? When it rises high enough, the water will short out their motherboards. They know everything—they must know that, too. He looks around for the rabbi but her eyes are closed. His chest floods with pity: for her or for Alisdair and Sadie or for himself, he can't say.

Checklist complete, Bob turns to bark: "Let's go." And then, in some spirit of wild abandon that must be brought on by the micro-mic outage, looks at Fantelle and him with disdain: "I don't know why we're even saving you two."

Bob stays on their heels and the three of them speedwalk through the empty units, making their way West to East. Then they're outside in the hot breeze. Transports do hyperspeed on the designated roads, but storms can take weird turns. Who knows whether they'll make it? The tornadoes might wipe you out before the rain ever starts. The light outside's begun to go a strange color—chartreuse? A whir of wings above: white ducks, a liberated farmful, hundreds of them.

The staff bus awaits them, the other crews already loaded up. Bob climbs aboard and Flint steps aside to let Fantelle follow: ladies first, or is that verbot? Fantelle does a neat swivel. In a flash, she's grabbed his hand and, before he can take in what she's up to, they're both hoofing it around the front of the autonobus. Once they clear the bumper, Fantelle lets go of his hand and heads full-throttle to the woods, but he's fully juiced and keeps apace for once.

Bob has no botsies to send after them. That gasping sound they hear behind them has to be Management Man himself, falling back farther and farther as Fantelle dodges under oak limbs and Flint crashes his way through the brush.

Eventually they stop hearing the choking sounds coming from Bob and pick the same beat to look over their shoulders. Bob's gone. He's retreated and left them to the storm. They slow—it could always be a trick—but finally, dimly, they hear the autonobus take off.

Fantelle still breathes hard: "I. Thought. They'd. Never. Leave."

He's breathless too, but manages a small whoop. "I reckon we're Swamp Foxes."

She gives him that raised eyebrow. "We can head back now."

"Back? Where?"

Her hair looks alive in the green light. "The unit."

He's dumbfounded. "The unit's going to flood. The botsies would kill us."

"They aren't coded for staff coming back."

"Exactly." Disbelieving, he stares at her scrunched face—Patsy's face, Hardy's—exhausted and irritated, flabbergasted at his stupidity. Now, when they finally have their freedom. Now, when he can finally make his moves. They have, what, an hour, maybe two, before they have to shimmy up a tree, lash themselves in. Even the rabbi got a hug. And after a hug . . .

"I have to get back to the rabbi," Fantelle says.

This stuns him all over again. "The rabbi can't shinny up a tree."

"What are you talking about?"

"The rabbi can't keep up with us. We have to lash ourselves to a tree—"

"That's absurd. No."

"Yes. With vines. You braid thick vines, then circle-tie." Something out of a book Patsy read: if they had to survive a superstorm, they could do it in the stoutest, oldest tree in the forest.

Her face de-scrunches. "That's ridiculous. I'm going back."

"Talk about ridiculous. You'll drown."

"I've survived supers."

And so, come to think of it, has he. But even if there's a chance they could survive in the unit, this is their shot at freedom, at a life in the woods. He's sure there are other resisters out here. There are always resisters. Mr. M gave them a long list: Yemassees, escaped slaves, draft dodgers, Iran War deserters. His father could be out here. "Look, if you do survive, they'll zap you for the rest of your life."

Her lean legs tremble at that, but her voice pitches stubborn. "The rabbi shouldn't be alone."

"Neither should I." Whose voice was that, sounding like ten-year-old Ricky Lee Flint? Their mother tried to prepare them for the removal, but there was no preparing. The b-guards surprised them in mid-day, while they were sleeping. Nell was just growing little breasts then. She used one hand to cover them under her nightgown, the other to touch the b-guard marching their mother away. To implore the unimplorable. He tries again: "Please. Stay."

"I can't." At least she says it kindly, almost as kindly as his mother promised to keep them in her heart. "I can't let her die alone."

He hears a primal groan rise up from his gut before a flash of fury overtakes him. The ground beneath their feet vibrates with snakes and insects and small critters burrowing deeper against the storm. Fantelle turns and walks away.

Don't! Maybe he just cried out or maybe he's only remembering. His mother didn't turn back to look at him and Fantelle doesn't either, only picks up her pace. There's still time. He's stronger: he could grab her wrist, pull her along until she changed her mind. Christ, whose caveman voice was that? *Don't worry, Fantelle, this won't hurt a bit.* He swings wildly. He could go with her, fight off the botsies single-handedly, sit by the rabbi until the waters receded. Then they'd all swim their way to freedom.

Maybe he's gone as shit-ass bonkers as she has.

Don't leave. He doesn't know whether he said that, either, but he knows what he sees, real as the shimmering ground or the electric air: the rabbi's head bent over her prayer, lips moving. He moves his own lips, and the words come unbidden. *Tell me what to do,* they say, and he doesn't know whether he's praying to the rabbi's god or the rabbi or the dim memory of his mother. *Don't let me die alone.* He scans the sky, the thick immobile wall of purple clouds that form a barricade between him and a direction. He can almost feel his legs start to pump, though which way they're moving he can't yet say.

ACKNOWLEDGMENTS

Warm thanks to these publications and their editors for initial publication:

Agni, "Our Last Stand."

Cabbage and Bones: An Anthology of Irish-American Women's Fiction, edited by Caledonia Kearns (Henry Holt), "The Other Woman"

Chicago Tribune Printers Row, "Suicide Dogs" (originally published as "Dog Suicides.")

Commonweal, "Company" and "Children of Night."

Image, "A Freak of Nature" and "Tidal Wave." Special thanks for the Pushcart Prize for "Tidal Wave," *The Pushcart Prize XLII,* 2018.

Prairie Schooner, "The Age of Infidelity." Special thanks for the Glenna Luschei Prize.

Ploughshares, "Sleepwalk." Special thanks to *The Pushcart Prize* for the "Distinguished" citation.)

Witness, "The Object of My Preposition." Special thanks to the Pushcart Prize for the "Distinguished" citation.

I am happily in the debt of countless friends and family who will receive their thanks in person but must acknowledge here the special generosity of Maria Tomasula, Gregory Wolfe, Sallie Vandagrift, William O'Rourke, Jesse Lander, and Margaret Doody, who first voiced a line about God sending all the intelligent life to other planets.

This book was set in Adobe Garamond, designed by Robert Slimbach, and based on the roman type of sixteenth-century typographer Claude Garamond and the italic type of Robert Granjon.

This book was designed by Shannon Carter, Ian Creeger, and Gregory Wolfe. It was published in hardcover, paperback, and electronic formats by Slant Books, Seattle, Washington.

The cover image is *When I Was You*, by Maria Tomasula, 2015, Lithograph with hand-applied watercolor on Rives BFK paper, edition of 45, 32 x 23 inches.